STILL HE KILLS

BRYAN MICHAEL ELLIS

ENCOMPASS INK

Dedicated to my oldest brother, Brett Ellis, who was taken away from this world much too soon, and to my mom, Reneé, who is my best friend and continues to believe in me.

CONTENTS

In the darkest of night,
Beneath the pale moonlight
You will pray,
For the light of day
Beneath the trees made of pine,
Chills will run up your spine
Sickle in hand,
Your death will be grand
Beware the mill,
For still he kills.

PROLOGUE

The foul stench of death filled the night air. Like rotten eggs covered in maggots, at least that is what Talia Masters imagined death to smell like. The young woman looked down at the dead rabbit that lied by her feet. Organs spilled out of its stomach and the poor creature's face was torn off. The pretty young blonde looked at her boyfriend, wondering how the hell she let him talk her into coming to this shit hole. Talia shivered as she stared at the old grist mill. It was no longer in use. It hasn't been for at least five years or so, probably more. No way was she going in there, no matter how much Lucas persuaded her to. The little mill stood over the stream, the giant water wheel still turning. The wood was rotting, and the roof was close to caving in. The sign sat on the ground, Cedar Creek Grist Mill.

A relic, she thought.

"Come on, babe!"

"Lucas, I told you. I'm not going in there. You've heard the stories."

He rolled his eyes and ran a hand through his thick dark

hair, which fell to his shoulders. He strutted towards the shorter girl and held her close. He kissed her forehead, the way a father would kiss a child. *I hate when he treats me like I'm a child and not his girlfriend.*

"Come on, we won't stay for long. I just want to see the inside of this place. We can tell everyone we went inside the old haunted grist mill."

Talia had no clue why he wanted to brag about something like that. *Such childish bullshit!* But for some sick reason, she didn't know, she loved him. He let go of her and grabbed her by the hand and lead her towards the small building. It seemed to fall apart before her eyes. Over his shoulder was a blanket. She felt as if she was about to enter the first lair of hell.

Inside the smell grew worse; it smelled road kill. Bugs flew around as she swiped them away. The door clicked behind them. The room grew small and Talia swallowed, her throat feeling dry. Being inside, made the bile rise in her throat and her stomach felt like it was sinking.

"Lucas, let's go," she whined. She felt like a child calling out for her mother.

"Come on, Talia."

He lied the blanket on the dirty floorboards and kneeled down, bringing Talia to him. Her light blonde curls bounced as she sat down on the soft fleece. He began to kiss her neck, sucking on the skin.

"Not here."

"Come on," he whispered into her ear. His voice, deep and sexy, always sent shivers up her spine. Lucas was walking sex, but at this moment, not even James Dean in the buff could get her excited.

His hand moved up to her small, but firm round breast. Talia let out a soft moan, her own desires betraying her. She could feel Lucas's boyish smirk against her neck. He thought she liked it, and maybe she did.

"Let's finish this at your place," she spoke.

He whipped his tee shirt over his head, revealing his smooth muscular body. As his jeans came off, he was left in his boxer briefs. She could make out the outline of his erection. He kissed her neck and slowly unbuttoned her blouse. She regretted not wearing a bra that day. With her breasts exposed, her nipples grew hard. She felt oddly exposed in this horrible place. As he lowered her onto her back, she fought the feelings that ran through her body. Her brain screamed for her to leave, while the rest of her body ached for an orgasmic sensation.

They were alone. She could go through with this, she told herself. He unbuttoned her jeans and as she felt his warm muscular fingers enter her, she moaned. He thrusted his fingers into her as she lowered his underwear. She grabbed his erection and together they made love to one another with their hands. For a moment she forgot where she was.

Creak.

She took her hand away and stood up.

"What the hell was that?"

"Talia, it's an old place. Old places make noises like that."

She shook her head and hugged her naked torso. He pulled up his underwear and hugged her.

"Nothing is going to get you while I'm around," he spoke. He kissed her lips and then smiled at her. They sat back down and begin to kiss again. Lucas crawled on top of Talia and kissed each nipple and down her body. Pulling down her jeans, she felt his tongue enter her.

"Oh, Lucas," she moaned. This all felt so good. She

closed her eyes and pretended they were somewhere else, like an engagement suite at a fancy hotel. The kind that served expensive liquor and had room service and waiters in tuxedos. Nothing like what they had in Cedar Creek.

Creak.

That was it! She pushed Lucas away and buttoned up her jeans. They had to get out of there.

"Talia!"

"It's time to go, now!"

She grabbed her blouse and turned around. Before she could close the first button, she came face to face with what looked like a monster! Towering over her stood a hulking beast of a man. She looked up and screamed. He wore a pair of tattered brown shorts, with a rope as a belt. His shirtless, muscular torso was dirty and covered in blood and mud. He wore leather boots, but worst of all was the mask he bore. She couldn't turn away from the black eyes of the mask as the face of a dead rabbit covered the top half of his face, while barbed wire wrapped around his head keeping the dead animal in place. One long ear still stood up, while the other flopped down.

In his hand he held a large, rounded sickle, stained with dried blood. The Miller swiped the sickle, catching her arm. She shrieked as skin ripped open and blood poured down her arm. Lucas screamed and ran for their attacker, but it was finished before he even knew it. The Miller grabbed Lucas by the head and brought the sickle to his neck and cut it deep into his flesh. He choked up blood, spitting it onto Talia's face, as the Miller worked the sickle back and forth like an old saw. He kept hacking as Talia screamed, until her lover's body fell to the ground, shooting blood from the stump of a neck. The Miller held his head by the hair and stared at it. She ran for the front door and the Miller gave chase.

Talia's fate was written the moment she stepped foot in those doors. She ran along the trail, ignoring the cold and the burning in her legs. She had to get back to the car. The Miller followed behind. Running after her, sickle in one hand, head in the other. He threw the man's head. It soared through the air and collided with the girl's back.

Talia screamed and fell to the ground. The killer stomped towards her and grabbed a clump of her hair and dragged her away. She screamed and kicked. She clawed at his bloody hands, but he never stopped. She felt like a rag doll being thrown around, her hair about to be ripped out.

The grist mill came back into sight and the Miller walked towards the giant wheel. He threw her head into the gears and she screamed.

"No! Please!"

The Miller turned the wheel, forcing it. Talia felt pressure in her head. Nothing like a headache. This was worse. She screamed, but the Miller used all his strength to push at the wheel and like a grape her head seemed to explode. Crushed beneath the wheel blood and gore spattered his mask and dripped down into the stream. Parts of the young woman's brain stuck to the mill like old food thrown at the wall. The water in the stream turned red.

CHAPTER

ONE

The small town of Cedar Creek was home to some, and Hell to others. The town was a quiet one, made mostly of farms and cornfields. Population: only a couple hundred. If that. And many of the couple hundred were full of hate. It came with the territory of a small town, Tyler Wuerth figured.

He hated this town. Born and raised in Cedar Creek, he knew of no other life, but no other life could be any worse than living in little Cedar Creek.

It was a hot May day as Tyler rode his bicycle through the small town. The wind swept at his blonde hair and he felt happy as he flew down the streets. He could be flying right now. He wanted to spread his arms out and take off into the sky, find himself a new home. Some place beautiful, possibly over the rainbow as Judy Garland once beautifully put it. He learned years ago life wasn't a movie.

He came to a stop outside the town's hardware store. He locked his bike and walked inside, hands in his pockets. He pushed his glasses up his nose and heard the small bell as he entered. It was a small store, carrying all the essentials that every farming town needed. Nicole Schaefer, wearing the red smock they were all forced to wear, waved at him as she used a small gray gun to place price stickers on sale items.

He clocked in at the register and walked to the stock room. He grabbed a lanyard with his name tag and another red smock to wear over his clothes.

"You're late," a rough voice spoke behind him. Tyler turned around to find the owner, Curtis Phelps, staring down at him with crossed arms.

"Only by a minute."

"You're still late. Get to the floor, before I write you up, again."

Tyler sighed and listened to his asshole of a boss, like he always did. He nodded and headed to the floor of the tiny store. He had no clue why Curtis had it in for him. He was never anything less than a model employee.

Actually, he had one idea why Curtis had it out for him, the same reason the rest of the town did.

He never wanted to come out, but it wasn't his choice. It was taken away from him, and now he was stuck in this daily cycle of torment. Even Hell couldn't be this bad.

The clock always seemed to slow down while he was at work. A second would turn into an hour and a minute would turn into a year. When he was at the hardware store, life slowed down to become a droll slog of a time. As a kid he always thought he would have a job he'd love where he would come in and be ready to take on the day, but instead he found himself stuck. Stuck in a job he hated. Stuck in a town that had long ago shunned him. Stuck in a life he didn't want. It's funny how life turns out.

He was nineteen and should be in college, but he was forced to work straight out of high school. He watched as some teens left the town, but most stayed behind to go on to live and die here like their parents once did. But then there were the ones who escaped, and Tyler found himself so envious of them. The thought that they had gotten away made him made him sick to his stomach. It wasn't fair they got to leave but he was the ones forced to stay behind. For now, he was stuck, but one day he'd make it out. His best friend always told him he was a survivor.

The hours ticked by, and when it was time to leave, Tyler raced out of there and jumped on his bike. He pulled on his headphones and hit play from his cassette player. As he sped through the town on his bike, he listened to Judy Garland as her vocals took over his world. The music played on and he was transported to another world, not one from this dimension. His black-and-white world became one of color. He was Dorothy landing in Oz. When the music played, his imagination went wild. He was living new lives and fulfilling new dreams. He was the hero of his imagination.

But all fantasies must come to an end.

He stopped outside the two-story farmhouse he hated to call his home. He let out a sigh of relief, when he didn't see his father's car. It wouldn't be long, but he would take advantage of the quiet. He parked his bike on the side of the house and unlocked the front door. He pushed his headphones down to his neck and walked into the kitchen. His stomach growled the moment he looked at the refrigerator. He opened the door, not seeing much. He had to go shopping soon, since his father didn't know what it meant to buy food. Only alcohol.

Fuck, what would he make for his father tonight?

He made himself a peanut butter and strawberry jam sandwich and brought it up to his bedroom. He closed his door and sat on his bed. He kicked his sneakers off, liking the sound of them falling softly onto the red carpet of his room. That little patter. His room was mostly bare. It lacked a personality. The red carpet was the most vibrant aspect. His walls were a light beige and red curtains decorated his two windows. No television, no posters, no trophies. Nothing was there to say a teenage boy lived in this room. There was a record player next to his bed and a bookcase on the opposite wall, right next to the wardrobe, and on the floor a basket could be found with old records. On the other side of his bed was a nightstand with a lamp and an alarm clock. To the left on the same table was a photograph of him as a child, around six or seven, with his mother.

He took a bite of his sandwich and stared at a picture of his mother. He ran a finger over her once young and pretty face. So many years ago, life seemed so simple, now everything has become a mess. It began when his mother died, but that wasn't the exact day his entire life turned to Hell. That was when he was seventeen in his junior year of high school and it happened in the gym's showers. Just the thought of that place sent a shiver through his body. There are some memories you don't want to remember, and then there are memories that you block. The kind of memories that while gone, could still hurt you. For Tyler this certain memory of the high school gym showers, was one he wanted to pretend never happened.

He heard the front door slam.

Shit! He's home! Be calm, Tyler. Be calm. Maybe he is in a good mood. I don't need to worry. Don't worry, yourself.

He took a deep breath and left the plate on his bed. Only one small bite was taken. He quietly opened his door and listened. Nothing was being thrown around. No drunken gibberish being thrown around. Maybe he was safe. God, he hoped he was safe. He prayed he was, but safe or not, he really wished his bedroom had a lock on the door.

He closed his door and went back to his sandwich but found his appetite has disappeared.

"Tyler!" the older man downstairs screamed. Tyler jumped in his bed, nearly biting his lip right through the skin. His stomach felt empty, but his throat burned with the sensation of lava forcing itself up.

"Tyler," he shouted again. "Get down here." Tyler stood up and made his way downstairs to the kitchen. His father sat at the table. His breathe reeked of whiskey. His baseball cap was stained with beer, and the flannel he wore smelled of vomit and cigarette smoke.

"Hello, Dad," Tyler greeted his father, his voice barely above a whisper. Frank Wuerth stood up and stared down at his boy. He grabbed his son's thin oval face in his hand and forced the ungrateful brat to look him in the eyes like a man.

"Be a man, Tyler. Not a fucking queer."

His father let go of his face and moved to the refrigerator and pulled out a can of beer. That's the only thing this fucking man ever bought for the house. Tyler did everything else with his own money.

"Did you hear what I said?"

Tyler nodded, "Yes, Dad."

"I can't hear you."

"Y-Yes, D-Dad," he spoke louder, a tremble in his voice and a sob caught in his throat.

His father smirked and stumbled over to the boy. He ran a hand through Tyler's thick blonde hair.

"That's my boy, Tyler."

He gripped his hair and pulled his head back. Tyler

cried out. Pain shot through his neck and head, the hairs threatening to rip out of his skull.

Please, let go! I beg of you! You're hurting me! Tyler stopped speaking his thoughts out loud years ago, when he realized it made everything worse. Please, stop. Stop! Stop!

"Now go make me some dinner."

He let go of the boy's hair. He didn't just let go, no, he threw the boy to the ground. Tyler's glasses fell of his face and as he reached for them, he thanked God they didn't break. His back stung from the impact against the floor. He looked up. His father was bathed in shadow, but he could still make out his cold brown eyes. He thanked the stars every single damn day that he looked nothing like his father.

"What do you want?"

"Do I need to tell you everything, boy?" His father lifted up his hand and Tyler closed his eyes and hid his face with a small squeak escaping his lips. Frank smiled. He grabbed his son's cheek and caressed it. His drunken haze of a brain was telling him it was time to sit in his recliner and watch the tube.

"I'm sorry, Dad."

"Now get yourself together, before I kick your ass, like the little Faggot you are." Tyler silently cried as his father walked into the next room. He stood up and without saying a word made his father dinner. All he could find was bacon, eggs, and bread. He made the eggs just how his father liked it, sunny side up (and with a little spit added in for extra flavor), the bacon burnt to a crisp, and the bread toasted black. He left the plate on the table and called the older man in. He might be his father by blood, but he'd never call him his father.

CHAPTER

TWO

The next morning, Tyler found himself standing outside of a bookshop. He entered the building, hearing the little ding of the bell welcoming him inside. It was a small shop in the shape of a square. Each wall was lined with shelves of books, with about ten aisles on the floor. Next to the front entrance was a desk with an old cash register set up and a dial phone beside the register. Angela Baker stood behind the register reading a gossip magazine. All of these brilliant novels inside, and the woman chose that trash. Tyler rolled his eyes. She looked up and glared at him. She was an older woman, early fifties, and quite large. Her head was round like a basketball with the wrinkles to match and her hair was short and curly. It was dyed black with visible gray roots. Her dress was too tight for her round body, with bulges of flesh popping out everywhere. Her rotund breasts were spilling out. One wrong move and the world would get a show.

He turned around and walked through the aisles of books. He used to consider this place a safe haven, but even here he was an outcast. Fuck this town, he thought to himself. Fuck this town and all the people that reside in it. He turned the corner of the aisle and his breathing stopped. Leaning up against a book case was one man he wished he could avoid for the rest of his life, Beau Hawthorne. They went to school together from pre-K all the way through to senior year. In a small town like Cedar Creek, it was impossible to avoid anyone. He backed away and walked past old bitchy Baker and grabbed his bike. He rode off. He's been trying to forget about his past, but that asshole had to pop up in the bookshop. Beau was not just one of the people to ruin his life, but he was the leading force behind his excommunication from the town. How could someone forget about their past, when it kept sneaking back into your life like a leech attaching itself to your body.

He rode his bike past the hardware store, past the library, past the small chain restaurants and diners. He kept pushing on the pedals until the buildings became scarce and it was all farmland. His face grew wet with tears. He also wished he didn't cry so much. Frank was right. He wasn't a man.

Just a faggot.

Across the town the sun shone down on the grist mill. In the daylight every crack could be seen. The windows weren't just broken, but they were nearly black with caked on dirt. Dust billowed inside like a heavy fog, but the giant wheel still spun over the stream. Inside the bodies of Talia and Lucas were sat up against the wall. His head was gone, and hers was crushed. Flies flew around their bodies. The man with the Rabbit face crawled into the room on all fours and stared directly at their bodies. He held the boy's head in his hands. He clutched it close to his chest, the way a child would hug a teddy bear. He sat in between their bodies and he tried putting the head back on the boy's stump, but it rolled off. The Miller tried again, but it fell to the ground. He jumped up and growled at the bodies, throwing the head to the ground. The dirty man hopped around like a dog, growling at the bodies.

He straddled the male corpse's body and unbuckled the jeans. He pushed them down and turned the headless corpse over. His buttocks were white and cold as the Miller shoved a finger inside. He smelled his hand and let out what sounded like a laugh, but not quite. More like the death screech of an animal as if it was being crushed to death.

The wild animal of a man held onto the head and placed it onto the woman's lap. The Miller took the girl's hands and placed them around the head, the way someone would hold their pet in their lap. Rabbitface caressed the girl's face, before patting her blood-stained hair.

Ethan Gardner worked on his parents' farm. His shirt was off, and the sun was blistering hot. His tanned skin baked beneath the bright yellow sun. He held a pitchfork in his hands as he stabbed his tool into the hay, moving it over to his red pick-up truck. His mother walked out with a tray of three glasses, while his little sister followed close behind.

"I have iced tea, Honey," Cynthia Gardner said. She had the kind of voice that could make a death threat sound sweet. The little nine-year-old girl, Grace grabbed a glass and smiled.

Ethan wiped the sweat off his forehead and stabbed the pitchfork into the earth. He grabbed a glass and took a long heavy sip. The cold liquid worked its way through his body, quenching his thirst and giving him a small chill.

"Thanks, Mom," he spoke. There was a Southern drawl to his deep voice.

"No, thank you so much for all the help you're doing on our farm. It's looking great again, just how it used to."

Ethan smiled. "It's okay. Dad is busy, but I've got it. You girls have nothing to worry about."

"My hero," Grace uttered with sarcasm dripping in her voice. Ethan finished off his iced tea and smirked. She looked up at her brother and wondered what the hell he was thinking. He ran at her and pulled her into a hug.

"Ew, you're all sweaty!"

Ethan and Cynthia laughed as he crushed his sister to his body. Grace shook her head and began to laugh too. Ethan let her go and turned his eyes to his mother. She put her glass down and backed away.

"No, Ethan!"

Ethan grabbed for his mother, but she jumped back and ran. The two laughed as he pretended to chase her. Grace shook her head embarrassed. Was this really her family?

"I need a shower now."

She took her iced tea and walked back into the farmhouse. Ethan leaned up against his truck and sat down on the bed of it. His flannel hung over the side of the truck.

"It looks like you have company," his mother said, picking up her glass again.

Ethan looked up the dirt road and saw Tyler and his bicycle working up towards the farm. He couldn't stop the smile that overtook his face. His heart pounded in his chest, and his sweat seemed to multiply. He smelled his armpits and grimaced. He'll just make sure not to lift his arms.

"Hello, Tyler," Cynthia greeted her son's best friend.

Tyler smiled. She was one of the few people who didn't act different towards him after high school. "Hello, Mrs Gardner."

"Would you like a drink?"

"No, thank you. I'm good."

"Okay, I'll leave you boys alone. I will be inside if you need anything."

She walked back towards the house. Tyler let his bike fall to the ground and Ethan helped him up onto the back of his truck. They sat there in silence and Ethan lost his smile. Something wasn't right. The air was heavy, almost suffocating.

If this has to do with his father, I swear I will fucking rip him apart with my bare hands!

"I'm glad you were home. This was pretty spur of the moment. I just had to get away for a little bit."

"Of course, what happened?"

Tyler sighed and looked down at the ground. His cheeks grew red and he bit his bottom lip. Ethan placed a hand on his back and rubbed soft circles, massaging the tense muscles.

"Tyler, talk to me, or I will have to force it out of you."

"And how do you plan to do that?"

"Well I know where you are ticklish, don't forget."

Tyler thought about it for a moment and opened up. "I ran into Beau."

Ethan clenched his jaw, feeling his teeth grinding in his mouth. He suddenly grew tense, taking his hand off Tyler's back. He stood straight up and licked his lips. His blood turned hot, like coal on a fire. His fists began to shake. He looked down not even realizing he made a pair of fists.

"Ethan," Tyler began.

"What did he say?" Ethan asked, his veins popping out in his neck.

"Nothing. I didn't really run into him. I saw him, and then I turned around. I don't even think that he saw me."

"You swear? He didn't do anything." Ethan's voice was nearly booming.

Tyler looked down at his feet, and Ethan's eyes softened. He grabbed his shoulder and apologized.

"I'm sorry, I really hate what he did to you. He's a bastard."

Ethan hugged Tyler, bringing him close to his sweaty muscular chest. Tyler was taller than him, but as he laid his head on Ethan's shoulder, he was able to breathe in his honey blonde hair that drove his senses crazy, opening in his mind the image of himself as a young boy picking little honeysuckles from his grandmother's garden. His smell brought him a sense of euphoria.

"Thank you, Ethan." His dark brown hair fell into his eyes. Tyler looked down into the man's light chestnut brown eyes. His eyes were rich and full of life. They had a hint of gold. Looking into those eyes made him no longer feel lost. Those eyes were the sweet whispers of love and childhood memories. They brought him a sense of safety. He breathed in his sweat, and even that smelt wonderful. Years of friendship and he was in love with his best friend.

"Come on, let's go into the barn."

Tyler nodded and followed him into the barn, the place they nearly grew up in. For years the two of them have escaped into this barn to be alone, talk the night away, and to open up and be free with one another. Ethan was the only person in Tyler's life who he could truly trust, and that was why he was in love with the gorgeous farm boy. Only a year older, Ethan seemed to have all the wisdom that Tyler wished he had.

In the barn, they lied down in the hay, backs up against the wall. Tyler rested his head on the older boy's shoulder, as Ethan placed his arm around him. They sat there in silence. He knew his best friend. Sometimes Tyler just needed silence. Too many people try to fill the air with nonstop chatter, when all someone needs is a shoulder.

"My dad is asleep now. I left him passed out on the couch."

"He doesn't know you left?"

"No."

"Do you want to sleep here? Slumber party?"

"As long as your parents don't mind?" Tyler's cheeks grew red. He still got embarrassed being around him, even after all these years.

"Of course not. My mom considers you family."

"Your dad isn't my biggest fan."

"He's not mine either. In fact, I think he likes you more than me." Ethan flashed a smiled and the two boys broke out in giggles.

How did he always manage to make Tyler feel good? Tyler could be on the verge of jumping off a bridge, but Ethan's presence could bring him back to the other side. Tyler felt Ethan's hand rubbing his shoulder.

Tyler wanted to kiss him. He wanted to kiss him so bad, but how would Ethan react. Tyler couldn't risk fucking up the only good thing in his life. Plus, he was a coward as his father told him nearly every day. A man like Ethan didn't deserve a scared boy like him, he felt. But as he stared at the face, that could have been chiseled out of stone by a God, he didn't care if he was good enough or not. He wanted to kiss him. He wanted to feel his full plump lips on his. He wanted those strong calloused hands to roam his body, the way he heard from girls how he used them. Tyler wanted Ethan to explore places no one else has ever dared to go. He wanted to make him feel good.

Tyler loved him, and always has. Ethan was the only man for him, and if he couldn't have him, he'd never risk losing his friendship. Even if it meant hiding his feelings.

THREE

Tyler hated to say it, but some of the best dreams he had, were the nights he dreamt of his father dying. Sometimes by his own hands. As he slept in Ethan's bed, only inches away from his body, he dreamt of his cruel father. In the dream he finally snapped and took a knife to his father's throat and slashed it open. It was a hunting knife, the kind with a serrated edge. In the dream he used the serrated edge, and really dug it into his neck. The little sharp pieces tore into the old haggard flesh of the man's throat, ripping it open. Tyler watched the blood spill out and smiled as his father choked to death on his own blood.

Tyler woke up to the sun shining through Ethan's opened window. Ethan was still asleep, lightly snoring. Ethan always denied he snored, but Tyler loved that he did. It was a cute snore. It was light, like the sounds of a newborn puppy learning to bark. Tyler watched Ethan sleep and looked down at his naked chest and the sparse dusting of light brown hair on his chest. Beneath the blanket, all he wore was a pair of tiny briefs, as did Tyler. That was the only layer that separated the two boys. Tyler grew hard at the thought.

Fuck! Not now, he thought. He tried to push his erection down, but as Ethan turned over, kicking the blanket down his body, all Tyler could see was the large bulge up front, and he grew harder. Fuck, he thought again. What am I supposed to do?

Tyler rolled onto his stomach and thought back to his dream and his father. Those dreams didn't just please him, but they scared him as well. Could he really kill someone? Yes, his father was cruel, but he was family. He beat him and made his life Hell, but he was also a living breathing man. Did he deserve to die? If he did, could Tyler really murder his own father? Or anyone at all?

"Good morning," Ethan said, sleep still in his voice. He rolled over to his side, pulling the blanket up to his waist. A light breeze came through the opened window above the bed. Tyler had spent most of his life in this very bed with Ethan. Years of pining, desire, and wanted to do so much more than just sleep beside him.

"Did you sleep okay?"

Tyler yawned. "Yeah. I slept okay. Thanks for letting me sleep over."

Ethan smiled, his eyes only half-opened. "Don't thank me. You can always crash here. You're my brother."

Brother.

"Okay," Tyler said.

Tyler closed his eyes and wanted to fall asleep again. Ethan may look at him only as a brother, but he would always be his savior to him.

. . .

In town, David Masters barged into the police station. His daughter hasn't been home in nearly two days now. She went out with that boyfriend of hers and never came home. Even the thought of the young man brought fire to his stomach.

"David, what are you doing here?" Deputy Erin Packard asked him.

"It's Talia. My daughter hasn't been home in two days. I called the other day, but some asshole said I had to wait forty-eight hours. It's been more than that, and I need you to help find my little girl!" His voice grew loud, but tears sat in his eyes.

"Come with me."

She led him to her desk and pulled up a chair for him.

"I need you to tell me everything that happened, David."

He nodded and started his story. His little princess was waiting for Lucas in her bedroom. She was getting ready, doing her make-up, when he knocked. She was always a daddy's girl, and he wouldn't have it any other way. He knew his wife was jealous of their relationship, but she is with another man now. Fuck her and her new man.

Talia knew of his disapproval of her boyfriend, and while he didn't condone it, he never stopped it either. He was a teenager once. He remembered when his parents tried to stop him, he rebelled harder. Talia would have to learn on her own. But if he got her knocked up, David would bring out his shotgun and shove it up his ass before pulling the trigger.

He finished telling his story to Deputy Packard.

"So, she was last seen with Lucas Langford."

"Yes. Now go arrest his ass. I know he had something to do with Talia's disappearance."

Erin read his pleading eyes. He wasn't just asking. He was begging her. She was his angel in that moment. She knew she'd have to find Talia, but she couldn't promise him either. Most of the time teenagers run away, especially if they have a boyfriend their father doesn't approve of. She could be shacked up with the boy right now.

"David, what brings you in here?"

Sheriff Michael Gardner walked up to Erin's desk. He was an older man with deep-set wrinkles and leathery-tan skin. He looked like a man who spent his life smoking.

"I'm here because Talia is missing."

"For how long?"

"Forty-eight hours," Erin answered.

"About two days," the frightened father answered.

Erin hated when people ignored her. Too many people assumed that because she was a woman, she didn't know what she was doing, but she wore her deputy badge for a reason. Erin stood up and walked outside as the two men spoke. Both men were nearly thirty years her senior. She was only thirty-three, but she wasn't dumb. She always wanted to be a cop. It was either that or lion trainer, but she didn't like clowns.

She got into her car and drove off to the Langford house. Talia's father was sick with worry, so why not find his daughter right away. She parked her car outside the trailer park and walked up to a small silver trailer. She knocked on the door. A fat older woman answered the door. Her robe barely contained her flesh and her hair was in curlers. A cigar dangled out of her mouth, with too much red lipstick.

"What do you want?"

"I'm Deputy Erin Packard with the sheriff's office in

town. I'd like to ask you a few questions about your son, Lucas."

The ugly woman narrowed her eyes. "What did my son do now? That lazy piece of shit."

"When was the last time you saw him, Mrs Langford?"

"Miss," she said stretching out the s like a snake. "And that would be two? No, three days ago? I don't know. He went off with that slut of a girl, Tanya."

"Talia."

"Whatever."

Erin took a deep breathe. Being around this woman was giving her a headache. Cedar Creek wasn't really known for their high-class society, but this woman gave white trash a new name. Miss Langford took a drag from the cigar and blew out the gray cloud of smoke. The smoke got into Erin's face. The old bitch laughed as Erin coughed.

"Oh, I'm sorry."

Erin knew she wasn't sorry. She had about enough of her. She handed over her card and asked her to call if she knew anything else. Erin drove off and the old bitch crumpled up the card and threw it onto the porch with a shake of her head. Like her husband, her son was a piece of shit. Good riddance, she thought. Good fucking riddance.

CHAPTER

FOUR

Days went by and still David heard nothing. What was the sheriff department doing to find his daughter? He knows his girl. She'd never runaway. She had no money and no clothes. Nothing was missing except for the clothes she wore that very day. Sheriff Gardner couldn't be bothered it seemed. David called every day and the sheriff grew angrier with each phone call. The angrier he became, the more desperate David grew.

If the sheriff wasn't going to do anything, then David would. He resided at a pharmacy using their copy machine. He watched as page after page, fliers flew out with Talia's face on it. He chose her high school yearbook photo. She always loved that one. She looked so beautiful. Like a movie star. Her big blonde curls were tamed in the picture and she wore a string of pearls around her neck. His girl was growing up, and he wasn't ready.

He took his fliers and left.

. . .

Kaitlyn Ward stood outside the gas station watching the numbers grow as she leaned against her car with the gas pump. Now where did the attendant say to go again? She was already forgetting the highway she was supposed to get off at. Driving from New York to Los Angeles might not have been her best idea, but she refused to regret it. She needed to think. The time to be alone. No men, no work, no worries. At least that is what she told her roommate before leaving the next morning. The pump came to a stop and she paid inside the station using her card. The attendant smiled. His two front teeth were missing. Kaitlyn smiled back and thanked him.

"Have a safe trip, Miss Ward."

Kaitlyn pulled on her sunglasses and turned around. "Thank you. Don't work yourself too hard."

Joey watched the girl drive away in her bright red convertible and wondered where the angel came from? There definitely weren't girls like her around here. His wife was nothing like her. She sat on the couch and watched television all day, while feeding their babies. Joey needed to get himself a city girl.

Kaitlyn drove with the top down, and her favorite cassette in the radio. Her long brown hair blew in the wind as she passed through the country. The farmhouses and the cornfields. The blue skies. The lakes. She felt like she was driving through a magazine. It was missing the heavy bustle of the city, but she was liking the quiet. She felt she could slow down, breathe in clean air, and relax. In New York, she was always on the movie. She moved fast, talked fast. Everything was telling her to go, go, go! But now, nothing was pressuring her. She slowed down the car and turned up the radio and laughed as Cindy Lauper performed along the open road.

Around the road was all cornfield. But in the distance was a small farmhouse. She lifted up her sunglasses and drove to the house. Kaitlyn stopped the car and turned down the music. She grabbed her camera and stepped out towards the house. Outside sat an old truck and the farmhouse had a wraparound porch with a swing by the door. The house was old. The once-white outside was turning brown. Next to it was a large red barn and a scarecrow stood erect in the field. The farmhouse with the blue sky and the bright sun behind, it was a painting come to life.

Kaitlyn aimed her camera and took a series of photographs. When she reached home, she would develop the photos in her dark room. There was something about the art. When she was in the dark room developing the pictures, she wasn't just reminiscing over a memory, but she was bringing to life a forgotten point in time. The one moment would live on forever. Life was fading, she knew that. She realized that in the past few months in her most recent epiphany, but photographs could make memories live forever. People disappeared into oblivion, soon to be forgotten, but photographs would always be around. Even after the human race ended, the photos would be proof that they were here. They were alive. They existed.

Tyler waited until his father was at work to come home. It was his day off and he wanted to take advantage of his alone time. He didn't have it often, but when he did, he wouldn't let it pass him by. He parked his bike outside his house and walked into the kitchen. He made himself a cup of tea and brought it up to his bedroom. He still wore his clothes from the day before, but they smelled of Ethan's sweat. Tyler breathed in the scent of his tee shirt before taking that first sip of tea. The hot liquid burned his tongue but quenched his thirst. Sipping the hot tea, brought back memories of the past slumber parties with Ethan. Since they were children they've been sleeping over one another's houses. Well, Tyler only slept over his friend's house now. After his mother's passing, Ethan didn't come over to his house anymore. Another thing he blamed on his father. His father didn't want to raise a queer, yet here Tyler was. His father failed, and now he was his disappointment to bare, like a soldier's guilt.

Last night he and Ethan were so close to one another. Tyler was almost in his arms, the ones he loved to be held in. The ones that made him feel safe. The arms that helped him forget about his father and this town and the shit-people who resided within it. If only he had the strength to tell Ethan how he felt, just to know his reaction. This secret was eating away at him, little by little. Each day he was losing more limbs to the pain. Tyler's heart was a firework, threatening to explode.

Tyler finished his tea and stripped off his clothes. He needed to relax. He placed a record on and let the music of Ella Fitzgerald fill the room. He had a few hours before his father was home. He grabbed a candle and a lighter and walked into the bathroom, adjacent to his bedroom. He left both doors open. As the bathtub filled with water, he listened to the melodic sound of her raspy, yet smooth voice. He lit the candle and added bubbles to the water. As the bubbles foamed, he turned off the water and sunk into the tub. He closed his eyes and breathed in the lavender scent of the candle and listened to the music. Everything disappeared for that moment. He felt tranquil. He let the water cover his body and his head. Beneath the water he descended. Tyler thought of the ocean. When he was young, and things were well. His mother was a live and his father wasn't an alcoholic. Everything was so simple back then. Nothing bad existed for him.

No cancer. No school. No sex.

It was the year before he started kindergarten and his parents took him on a trip to San Francisco. Tyler didn't remember much about his mother. Her memories were fading. Sometimes he had trouble picturing his mother's face. He remembered her hands. When she played piano, her fingers didn't just hit keys, but they glided over them. He remembered her voice. She had a lovely voice and would sing to him every night before bed. Sometimes she'd play the piano and sing for their guests. Tyler's father would watch proudly.

Alexandria Wuerth was an artist, and on that day in San Francisco, as they sat on the beach, Tyler remembered her fingers as she held him, and she sang to him. His father slept, his skin turning red, while his mother protected him underneath the umbrella. She sung a lullaby into his ear, tears in her eyes. Her tears soaked his face, and Tyler realized years later that she knew she was dying in that moment. If he had known then what he knew now, he would have relished every moment with her. He was so young. So dumb. Maybe nothing ever was simple. Childhood was a ruse, disguised to hide life's most brutal moments.

Closing his eyes, he let his tears fill the water. He was Alice in the room filled with her giant tears. He was swimming in the bathwater and tears. Nearly drowning in them.

He lifted his head from beneath the water and lied back, his head against the wall. Memories. It seems all his happiness resides from memories. Memories of his mother. Memories of a loving father. Memories of a childhood. Memories of a time before everyone knew he was gay in this town. Thank the shooting stars for Ethan, Tyler thought. Thank the stars.

ETHAN WORKED OUTSIDE on the farm while his father was at work and his mother and sister were out visiting a neighbor, but in this town the closest neighbor could be four miles away. That's how long Tyler traveled on his bike to him last night. He hated how Tyler did that. It was dangerous, especially at night. For four miles he was alone on that scrap of metal, which gave him no protection. He really wished he would call him when he needs a ride, and each time he told that to him, Tyler responded the same way. He didn't want to be a bother. After years, Ethan gave up. How long would it take to convince Tyler he'd never be a bother to him. He loved him more than anything life offered. Even more than his pick-up truck and cowboy boots.

He always liked when Tyler slept over. Sometimes Tyler fell asleep first, and Ethan always enjoyed watching him sleep. He lived his life in fear, and when he slept, he was innocent. He reverted back into a child and Ethan wanted to care for him like his son. He smiled at the image of Tyler sleeping in his bed. He looked angelic last night as the moon shined through his window, casting a luminescent glow upon Tyler's shirtless body. He's been having these thoughts for years now. Was it normal to call your best friend, who is a guy, angelic? Well, they were best friends. Brothers, really. They even shared blood. They have ever since they took a blood pact as children. They cut open their hands and held them together. They each still wore the deep score on their palms. Ethan remembered how pissed off their mothers were. Their fathers laughed, but he swore their mothers were ready to disown them in that moment. He laughed at the memory to himself. He thanked God for his mother and his sister. They took Tyler in like a second son, but he wished his father wasn't so hard on him. Ever since the outing, the sheriff seemed to have turned his back on the boy. Apparently having a gay man in your house was akin to having a contagious disease. Get to close and you catch the gay.

Am I gay? This is a thought that ran through his mind from time to time. He was always popular in school. He dated girls, even slept with a few, but none of them made his blood boil or his heart skip. None of them took his breathe away, but Tyler, made him feel something. When he thought of his best friend, his heart grew heavy and his body felt electric. He knew Tyler liked him, but Ethan never let on that he knew. He couldn't risk embarrassing his friend or losing him. Tyler thought of him as a hero, but Ethan was the man he was today because of Tyler. He was his rock, his person.

His everything.

CHAPTER

FIVE

David has had enough now. It's been over a week and the sheriff hasn't done shit. He has been posting fliers all over the town, and the sheriff hasn't even called him with an update. Nothing. He barged into the office and demanded to speak to the sheriff.

"David, sit down. Relax," said one of the younger officers.

David grabbed onto the desk, his knuckles turning white. His eyes narrowed, and he laughed. The officers looked at one another, almost scared of the desperate father.

"Relax? You think I should relax? Don't tell me to fucking relax when no one is looking for my daughter out there? It's been a week and a half, so I demand to speak to the sheriff. Now!"

The young officer before him nodded and walked into the sheriff's office. Erin was the only one not there. She was the only who gave a shit, David realized. Michael walked out and pulled him into his office. He shut the door behind him.

"What the fuck do you think you're doing? I should haul your ass in jail for that display out there."

"You think I should be in jail? That's great. Priceless, coming from you. What have been doing to find Talia?" David threw a flier onto his desk. "Look at her face! A week and a half. It's been ten fucking days, and I've heard nothing from you. You're a pathetic excuse for law enforcement."

"Now, you hear me, David. I won't take this kind of shit from some lowlife trash. Don't tell me how to do my job. I'm doing it just fine, you hear? Talia is probably just shacked up with that boy of hers, who also is missing. They ran away to be away from you."

David could kill the man right there. He could take the gun and shoot him right there. He'd plead insanity. Instead he pounded his fist against the wooden desk.

"Since the law in this town is shit, I will do something then."

He ran out of the building and jumped into his car. Enough was enough.

Work was busy for Tyler that day. He and Nicole were running around. The pay sucked, but it was something. It's the reason why he put up with the abuse from Curtis. Curtis was always an asshole, but when he was outed, he turned sadistic. Even today, he worked his ass off, and still the older man berated him. By 3pm, the store was slowing down, and Tyler took the moment to catch his breathe.

"You okay?"

He looked up to find Nicole staring at him. Her hair was pulled back in a bun and sweat dripped down her face. Tyler nodded, shooting her a small smile.

"Yeah. I'm wiped."

"Same here."

Curtis walked up to the two of them and groaned, as if he was in physical pain. "Get back to work."

"No one is here, Curtis," Nicole said.

"I don't want Tyler distracting you."

"But I'm the one..." Before she could finish, Curtis put his hand in front of her face. That means he didn't want to hear it. He walked away.

"Asshole!" she spit. Tyler giggled. "If we were smart, we would quit."

"Why don't we then?" he asked.

"Because then we'd have no money to survive. I fucking hate this greed-entitled world we are forced to live in. Like I get we need a system or whatever, but couldn't we just go back to bargaining or something?"

"Like you give me two cows in exchange for my shoes?" Tyler laughed. Look at him! He was actually laughing at work.

"Yeah, something like that."

The day went on like that. They would laugh, and Curtis would put a stop to it. It was like any other day. As they were getting ready to close that night (5pm every night), a woman walked in. She was browsing through the garden seeds. Nicole was ringing up an old man who owned a farm on the edge of town. Tyler walked up to the woman. She was older, but not old. Probably early thirties, he thought. She was skinny and what most men would find attractive. She wore little make-up and had her brown hair tied back in a ponytail. Her hot pink hoodie nearly blinded his eyes.

"Hey there," Tyler greeted. "Is there anything I can get for you?"

The woman looked right into his eyes, with a scowl on her face. She shook her head and rolled her eyes and turned her head away. Tyler took a deep breathe. Why did people feel the need to act like that? What gave them the right to act like they're above others. He wanted to grab the woman and shake her by the shoulders but took another breathe and just smiled instead.

"Well if you need anything, I'm Tyler."

"Whatever," she retorted.

"You're welcome," Tyler answered. The woman looked right up at him and her scowl became a snarl. She sucked in her cheeks and pursed her lips, her hands on her slim hips.

"Excuse me?"

"What?" Tyler asked.

"You know very well I didn't say thank you."

"I'm sorry, I thought I heard you say that."

The woman walked up to him and moved her purse to her other shoulder. She looked him up and down, licking her lips. She looked up into his eyes.

"You know I didn't."

"Ma'am, I really did. I apologize."

"Oh please! Where is your manager?"

His heart dropped, and the world stopped moving. He couldn't let her complain about him. Curtis was looking for any excuse to fire him. He didn't even hear Curtis show up beside him.

"What's the matter, Connie?"

"This young man was nasty to me! I was shopping, and he came up to me and was giving me an attitude."

"I'm so sorry, I will definitely do something about this. I'd hate to lose your business."

Connie smiled at the boy. She was the queen of her own life. She always got her way. Always did.

"She's lying!" Nicole spit. She left the register and joined the group. "I heard the whole thing. She was the nasty one. Not Tyler!"

"Shut it, Nicole. Tyler, go home. Nicole and I got it from here."

"But…"

"Now."

Tyler nodded, closing his eyes. He ripped off his apron and clocked out in the backroom. As he walked past the woman, his bag on his shoulder, he heard her mutter under her breathe, *faggot*. Tyler stopped in his tracks and turned to look back at the girl. He opened his mouth. He had to say something, anything. He couldn't go on letting people treat him like this in this town.

He turned around and left. He jumped on his bike and went home. No, he couldn't go home. His father was there. He pedaled in the opposite direction and went towards Ethan's house. Ethan had all the answers and always knew what to do in any situation. If he had been there, Tyler was sure Ethan would have come back at her with a retort back. Ethan didn't take shit from people, like Tyler did. Ethan had a backbone.

Tyler found Ethan alone on the farm. He was shirtless, but when wasn't he? Tyler's friend seemed to be allergic to shirts, not that Tyler minded. Ethan was washing his truck. Sweat ran down his body as he soaped up the car. Tyler threw his bicycle to the ground and walked up to Ethan. He turned around and saw the blonde pushing his large round glasses up his skinny nose.

"Hello there!" Ethan let the sponge sit on the hood of his car and he leaned against the faded red door. The paint was chipping off. "What do I owe the pleasure of seeing you here today?"

"Another shitty day at work."

"Let's go into the barn."

Tyler followed Ethan inside the barn and the two boys sat on the hay, backs against the wall. They sat in silence. Tyler didn't want to talk. He just wanted to be. Ethan squeezed his shoulder and rubbed his back. Tyler closed his eyes felt the hand slip beneath his shirt. Ethan's hand burnt his skin, but Tyler never wanted to lose the feel of him.

"That feel good?"

Tyler forgot how to form a word. All he could do was nod. His soft full lips were slightly opened. He licked his thick bottom lip, before biting the side. He had to stop biting his lip. Sometimes he'd bite so hard, his teeth would break the skin.

Tyler grew hard from the feel of Ethan's hand running soft circles on his back, massing the few muscles he had.

"Do you remember Jena Mink?"

Tyler nodded. She was a blonde cheerleader who went to Cedar Creek High with them. She was in Tyler's grade.

"Well we were assigned to work together on a class project. It was science. No, history, I think? Well it doesn't matter. What I was saying is she came to my house, wearing this sexy outfit. Tiny skirt, low-cut top. She was a teenage boy's wet dream."

Where was he going with this?

"So, she came over and we were in my bedroom working on the project, and suddenly her hand went for my dick. She started to rub it, and she unzipped my jeans, and pulled it out. I was hard as a goddamn rock."

Tyler watched Ethan's hand glide down his muscled body and beneath his jeans. Tyler watched, his breathing growing fast. Faster than his heart at that moment. His cock throbbed beneath his pants.

"Did she make you cum?" Tyler asked. A blush rose to his cheeks. The word cum made him squeamish. Well, talking about sex in general did.

"She did." Ethan was practically moaning as he pushed his jeans down. Tyler's blue eyes grew wide as Ethan's hard cock popped out. He watched his best friend jerk off. Ethan looked over and smiled. "You're hard too."

Tyler nodded, pushing his pants down. Together the young men masturbated, the only sounds filling the barn their slight moans.

"Do you mind if I try something?"

Tyler nodded. His mind was in overload. Ethan grabbed his dick and Tyler couldn't stop his loud moan. His dick grew harder in Ethan's grasp as he slowly worked it. Tyler grabbed Ethan's erection and did what Ethan did to him. Ethan's moans were lower but hearing his friend's ecstasy pushed him on.

Tyler looked down at the large penis in his hand. He wanted to make Ethan cum. No, he needed to make him cum. He had to be the reason of his pleasure. Just this once. He placed a small kiss on each one of Ethan's nipples, catching him by surprise. Ethan's nipples grew hard and he choked out a sigh as Tyler's mouth covered his erection.

"Fuck!"

He lightly rubbed the top of Tyler's head. Should they be doing this? Jerking off together was one thing, but now his best friend was sucking his cock. And he liked it. His mouth felt so good on him.

"Tyler," he whimpered. This was like no blowjob he had ever received before. It was so much more intense. "Tyler, you're going to make me, oh God. Fuck!" With a loud cry, he unloaded his seed into Tyler's mouth, watching him swallow every drop. Tyler sat back up, with a small smirk. He wiped his mouth with the back of his hand.

"Wow," Ethan said.

"Yeah."

Ethan pushed Tyler back down and he wanted to return the favor. He too, took his best friend's length into his mouth. Only the tip. Slowly he took more of it into his mouth, trying to find the right rhythm. He's never gave a blowjob before. It was weird. It felt like his jaw was locking and he was trying to eat but couldn't swallow. Almost as if he was choking, but it was a good choking. He listened to Tyler's whimpers, and took him seed into his mouth as Tyler orgasmed. He pulled his lips off and sat up. He looked into Tyler's eyes.

What did they just do? What did he just do?

"Tyler," he started. The sounds of a car pulled up to the house. Quickly the boys jumped up and pulled their pants back on. They looked at one another, saying nothing. What could be said? Should they feel guilty? Regretful? Happy? Sad? Their minds were swimming in chaos. How was it possible to feel so much at the same time? How could someone be both happy and sad?

"I should go."

Ethan didn't move. He stood still in the barn as Tyler jumped on his bike and zipped off. Ethan ran a hand through his hair, heavy with sweat. He felt something in his chest. His heart felt light and his stomach was empty. He felt good.

SIX

Frank was waiting for his son at home. All fucking day he worked. Why? So, he could support the brat and himself. He threw his beer bottle into the sink and opened another. Fuck! The little Fag didn't appreciate anything. Where was his dinner? Not here, and neither was Tyler. The kid wasn't his son. He was some stranger the woman popped out.

The door opened, and Tyler found his father sitting alone in the kitchen. Frank turned towards the boy.

"You're late."

"I'm sorry, I was working."

"The hardware store closes at 5pm. It is now after 6. So tell me where were you?"

Tyler's body shivered in the warm kitchen. Even the opened window couldn't stop the summer heat from seeping inside the house.

"I was with Ethan," Tyler answered staring outside. Fireflies were flying outside beneath the sun. Soon it'd be dark, and they'd be lighting up the night. Tyler always liked to imagine they were tiny fairies. His mother once told him if you catch a firefly, it would grant you a wish. Tyler has never been able to catch one.

"You were with Ethan."

"Yes, Dad."

"Did you two fuck?"

"What? No!" His father didn't need to hear the part about the blowjobs in the barn.

Frank stood up from his chair and walked over to his son. Tyler was tall, but Frank still towered over him, his fat belly straining the fabric of his wife-beater. Appropriate name for his shirt, Tyler thought.

"You two are always hanging around one another. Having your sleepovers like a pair of girls. It's funny, because I remember your mother having a son. I guess I was wrong. I have a daughter. I should buy you a dress and make-up. You'd like that. You make me sick." He finished off another beer and threw it into the sink. He walked to the refrigerator and opened another. As he opened it, he let out an earth-shaking belch. "Fags, both of you."

"Don't talk about him like that!"

"What did you say to me?"

Tyler closed his eyes and backed away. "Nothing."

Frank smiled. The pansy was almost a real man right there. He pulled off his belt and folded it.

"Say it again."

"I said not to talk about Ethan like that. He my best friend. He's more of a man than you'd ever be!"

The moment he said it, he felt his life was coming to an end. Time froze and that moment, that second became a lifetime. Regret. Sorrow.

Frank grabbed his son and threw him against the table and whipped his belt onto his body. With each pelt, Tyler cried out. When would his nightmare end?

. . .

ETHAN SHOWERED and thought of Tyler and what they had done in the barn. Ethan never thought of himself as gay, but being with Tyler in that way, felt right. Like two puzzle pieces connecting. He still liked girls, he thought. Maybe he was bisexual? He believed that was the term, but no girl has made him feel the way Tyler did. He wasn't just his best friend. He was something more. He could say lover, but that didn't seem strong enough of a term. Best friend. Lover. He was both and so much more to him. Was he in love with him? Has he been in love with Tyler all along?

He always loved Tyler. He was his best friend and his brother. But in love with him?

Ethan turned off the water and dried himself off. He wrapped a towel around his waist and walked to his bedroom, locking the door. Still thinking of Tyler, he let the towel fall to the ground and lied on his bed. He still thought of the barn. They've jerked off together before. Didn't all guys do that? Yeah, but they never jerked one another off before. He wanted to make his friend feel good, and instead made him cum in his mouth.

Ethan liked it too. He loved taking in the taste of his best friend and loved holding him. He wanted to do it again, he realized, but he was afraid he fucked up their friendship.

AS ETHAN THOUGHT OF TYLER, Tyler lied down in his own bed thinking of Ethan. Was he into him as well? Was that a one-time deal? What was that? Tyler's mind was an ocean of thoughts and questions, and he was swimming through it.

What? Why? How?

He was glad it happened, but he also wished it didn't. What if Ethan never looked at him the same way again? What if he cast him off? What if he met a girl...His head pounded with the start of a migraine. An aching pain pulsed in his head like the beating of his heart, becoming stronger and louder.

At the same time, it was a dream come true. He's been in love with his best friend for at least ten years, before he even realized he was gay. Maybe it was worth the chance? Maybe something could happen between them? Maybe he would lose him as a friend...

Maybe.

Maybe.

Maybe.

That was all his mind could ask. Maybe the world could end next week. Maybe he would be hit by a car tomorrow while riding his bike. The world was a series of maybes, but hardly any answers. A person just wanders through life, lost, unknown to what to come or where they were. Like Red Riding Hood lost in the woods.

Frank sat in the kitchen, beer in hand, and passed out. Working in construction took a lot out of him. He was exhausted. All life had left his body. After whipping the boy, he took another beer and passed out on the kitchen table. As he slept, his wife came to him in the dream. His once beautiful wife. His love. When he drank, he sometimes saw her. He would see her in the corner of his eye or in the face of a girl on the street. When one is drunk all the time, anything could be possible.

Anything.

So why stay sober? Sobriety was the cold hard proof he was nothing. He was a lousy husband. He is a lousy father. He is a sorry excuse of a person. When he became sober, he'd realize what has become of him, but once he drank, nothing mattered. The kid would be better off with another family.

His snores filled the kitchen, echoing through the house and into Tyler's bedroom. Tyler sighed, feeling relief. Nothing more could happen to him tonight. Once his father slept, he wouldn't wake up for anything. Not even if they started dropping bombs on the town. Now he was alone and safe, and all he wanted to do was see Ethan again. Yes, he wanted to take him into his mouth again, but he needed to see him like the man was his only source of air. He would suffocate without Ethan in his life. He knew he would. Tyler was the reason he was still here.

After his outing, Tyler fell into a despair, so deep, he was drowning. No matter where he was, he felt like the world was pulling him down, suffocating him. He couldn't breathe. He couldn't live. He couldn't handle it anymore. One day he came home and stared at the straight razor his father used to shave. He cleaned it and took it to his bedroom and he sat on his bed, with the razor before him. It lied on the bed taunting him, telling him to pick it up and end it all. It would have been so easy. He got so far as bringing the blade to his wrist, but he never pushed down. He couldn't. Something told him not to give up yet.

Don't give up. Keep going. You'll make it. A voice in his head repeated the mantra. Tyler almost believed it. Could he truly make it in this life? What if things only got worse? He was only a junior in high school and hated by everyone, including his father. The only person he had was Ethan, but he was a year old and was preparing to graduate. That would leave him one year alone in that place. He couldn't.

"I'm sorry," he whimpered. Tears fell in streams down his cheeks. He took off his glasses that moment and wiped them away. Again, he pushed the blade onto his wrist, but this time he didn't stop himself. His guardian angel did.

"Tyler, no!"

Ethan stood in the doorway staring with his mouth open. He ran to Tyler and ripped the blade out of his hand. Tyler didn't even break the skin. He couldn't even kill himself right. Ethan grabbed his shoulders and shook him. His eyes pleaded with his.

"Why, Tyler, why? Are you stupid?" he yelled, starring into Tyler's big blue eyes. With the tears, they appeared to him to be oceans. Ethan felt tears well up into his eyes and he pulled Tyler into a tight hug, squeezing his arms around him, hearing the bones crack in the boy's back.

"Why?" Ethan repeated.

"I'm sorry," Tyler muttered.

Ethan had hugged him that night. All night. He called his mother and slept over in Tyler's bed, holding him. He couldn't let his friend die. At the time, Tyler was full of guilt, sadness, and anger. How could he have done what he did? How stupid was he to even contemplate suicide, but he was also angry with Ethan for saving him. He didn't know how horrible his life had become. Ethan always had to be his knight in shining armor, but that one time, Tyler didn't want to be rescued. But he was glad to sleep in his best friend's strong arms.

Now he was thankful. He was glad Ethan stopped him from pushing that blade into his wrist. The voice in his head was right. He could make it. He would survive. Once he saved up money, he'd get out of the hick town. Maybe he'd move to a big city or live on his own in the woods. Just somewhere away from the daily torment and the vehement homophobia. Somewhere far away.

Perhaps somewhere over the rainbow.

SEVEN

K aitlyn checked into the motel at 11:30 pm. She was beginning to fall asleep at the wheel and the rain was coming down rather hard. If she didn't stop, she would be good as dead before the break of dawn. She found a small motel on the side of the road. It wasn't exactly the Ritz, but it would do. She took her bags inside and checked in. A terribly skinny young man stood at the front desk. Kaitlyn wondered when the last time he ate. Dark shadows surrounded his eyes and his cheekbones jut out like tiny knives beneath his skin. The sweater, he wore, was loose on his body, falling off one shoulder. He was a nice man. A sad man, she felt.

"Welcome! Are you looking for a room?" he had asked with a large yellow smile.

Kaitlyn smiled back, "Yes I am. Just for myself."

"How long would you be staying?"

"Just the one night," she responded.

"Oh," he answered with a sigh. His smile disappeared for a second but returned after a second. If she blinked, she would have missed the falter in his performance. He must have been so lonely.

He grabbed a key off the wall and she followed him outside to the first motel room. She thanked him and offered a tip but said he couldn't take it. He just wanted her to have a good stay. As Kaitlyn shut the door behind her, she wished more people in the world were like this man. Not enough good people out there. Her ex wasn't one of the good ones. One of the many things she was running away from. She hated to admit she was running away, but wasn't that essentially what she was doing? She told everyone she was just trying to find herself, but she was a liar. She lied like everyone else in the world. Perhaps she wasn't that good of a person?

She unloaded her bag and took a shower before bed. As she cuddled up beneath the blankets, she pulled out a journal from her side bag. Inside, she didn't write; instead were pictures she had taped into the journal. She smiled at the memories she had captured over her twenty-seven years of life. As she turned the pages, she was flooded with memories, both happy and sad, but mainly happy. She was greeted by pictures of her family, her friends, even her photography.

And pictures of Dustin. She shut the journal. She has had enough of memories for the night. She wished to take his pictures out, but something stopped her from doing so, as if she liked torturing herself by seeing his face. She stuffed the book back into her bag and turned the light off. It was time to sleep, before the memories haunted her anymore that night.

. . .

DAVID STOOD outside on the sidewalk of the police station, holding a stack of fliers. Two weeks it has been now, and still nothing. Where was Talia! He was becoming more and more desperate. Life was dripping away from him. His job ceased, and the food grew spoiled in his house. He lived on whiskey and bread. His face grew rugged with stubble and his hair was in need of a brush. He wore the same outfit from the day before. He couldn't remember if he showered. All he wanted was to find his daughter. He couldn't live until that was done.

He handed fliers out to anyone who walked by him. One officer told him to stop, but David ignored him and continued on with his tirade. He was on a mission. He was going to do what they couldn't do. He was going to find his girl. He was going to take his baby back home. He just knows that Langford boy did something. He either hurt her or convinced her into a life she didn't belong in. No matter what mistakes she made, David was going to hug her and do anything she wanted. Each night he cried himself to bed, unable to take the pain. His heart was being carved apart by a large knife each day his daughter was missing. But no breakthroughs.

Well none until the early afternoon of a hot June day. A girl walked up to him, biting her lip, with her eyes cast down to the ground.

"Mister Masters?"

"Yes." His intense eyes frightened the young woman. She really hoped she was doing the right thing.

"I think I know what happened to your daughter."

David's heart nearly gave out. Was he imagining those words? Was this girl really standing there. She seemed to be Talia's age. Perhaps they went to school together. He grabbed her shoulders and stared right into her.

"Tell me! Please! Tell me!"

The girl took a gulp and spoke. "My brother told me that she and Lucas went out to the grist mill that night she disappeared. The one people say is haunted on the edge of town."

"Thank you so much!" He hugged the girl and ran down the street. It was time to bring his princess back home.

Baby, Daddy's coming for you!

BACK AT THE grist mill on the edge of town, the Miller stood at the broken window and stared outside. The sky was growing dark and the earth was turning a shade of dark blue. The sun was beginning to set as a car came to a stop outside the mill. A man with graying hair and premature wrinkles stepped out of his car. In his hands were dozens of fliers with Talia's face on it.

The Miller watched the older man walked towards the grist mill. He tilted his head and disappeared into the shadows. David entered the mill and called out for his daughter. He knew she wouldn't be here, but he hoped. It had been nearly two weeks since she disappeared. He couldn't give up hope. Not yet. Not until he had his answers.

"Talia," he called out, "it is Daddy! Are you here?" No one answered, and he was not surprised. He knew that little weasel did something to Talia and he was prepared to kill him with his own hands. What did she see in Lucas? He had no job, a record, and a reputation that couldn't be beat.

A squeal came from the next room. David walked towards the sound, the floorboards squeaking beneath his weight. It sounded almost like a pig.

Or was his daughter hurt?

"Talia!"

David ran into the next room but found no one. Talia wasn't here, and the hand of hope lessened its grip on his heart. He begged for her to be okay and he had prayed to God for her safety, but still she hasn't returned to him.

David turned around and screamed. He found his daughter, except her head was crushed and gore and blood dripped down her body. This couldn't be true. Not after all this time. Not after his work. She couldn't be dead.

"My baby!" he screamed. He dropped all the fliers and ran to the girl. He bent down on the ground and picked her up and cried. Her blood stained his clothes, but he didn't care. He breathed in her dirty hair and sobbed into it. He rocked back and forth as if he was on an invisible rocking chair and Talia was a newborn again. Her eyes stood wide open and her body was beginning to rot. His head thought of nothing, becoming a black haze of dark smoke and his heart grew hollow. Nothing was in his chest.

Behind the man, out of the shadows, the Miller appeared like a ghost. The Miller let out a deep squeal and David turned around. The Miller raised his sickle and brought it down into the top of the strange man's head. It ripped out through his eye socket, the eyeball speared onto the point of weapon.

The Miller ripped the sickle out of his body and it crumpled to the ground next to his daughter. The eyeball rolled towards the Miller's feet. He bent down and sniffed it like a dog looking for dinner. He poked at the eyeball and crushed it beneath his boot. The eye made a sickening squish, the same sound of an insect being crushed.

EIGHT

Tyler was walking home late at night as he passed by the Gardner farm. He walked his bike. He had to escape his house. He couldn't be around his father tonight. If he was around him any longer, he'd do something he'd regret. It has been days since the barn. Days of silence and days of questions. Did Ethan regret what they did? Tyler knew he really fucked up this time. He probably ran off the only friend he had. But he had to be near him tonight, so here he found himself walking past the home of the Gardner family.

He looked up to find Ethan's light on in his bedroom. Tyler looked up and saw Ethan shirtless and sweating lifting his body up on a pull up bar. His muscles tightened, and his abs clenched. Tyler smiled at the sight of his best friend. His heart felt fuller as he looked up through the window. Ethan jumped off the bar and stretched his arms, before pulling down his workout shorts. Tyler bit his lip as Ethan stood there in in his boxer briefs. He felt as if he was intruding on his privacy, but he couldn't look away. His heart pounded in his chest wanted to see more, while his brain told him to turn back. The barn must remain a one-time thing, he thought.

Ethan looked down and Tyler's stomach sank. For a minute, they stared into one another's eyes, before Tyler turned around and ran. He fucked up. He shouldn't have come out here. He shouldn't have been watching his best friend, who called him a brother. Shit! He hoped he didn't ruin anything! He couldn't bare losing Ethan as a friend.

"Tyler, wait!"

Tyler stopped running and turned around. Ethan had on a tee shirt and shorts. Tyler apologized, "I'm so sorry. I was walking home, and I just happened to look up. I didn't mean to see." Tyler felt like a stalker.

"Do you want to see the real thing?"

"What?" There was no way Tyler heard him correctly. His mind was playing tricks on him. That was all.

"You heard me." Ethan had a shy smile on his lips. Tyler nodded, unable to find the words. Ethan grabbed his hand and lead him back to the empty house. His parents were out, and his sister was having a sleepover at a friend's house. Ethan lead Tyler to his bedroom and sat him down on the bed before locking the door.

As Ethan stripped off his shirt, Tyler sat there and watched. His eyes grew wide and he couldn't stop thinking of their time in the barn. Ethan licked his lips, enjoying the sensations he was giving his best friend. The tease was best part, an ex-girlfriend once said, and now he understood what she meant.

Tyler shivered in the small hot bedroom. Slowly Ethan pulled down his shorts and underwear, turning around. He wanted Tyler to see him, to truly see him. All of him. He looked back and smiled. Ethan was never much of a dancer, but he moved his hips in an easy rhythm. He was the charmer and Tyler was his snake.

"Do you like what you see?"

Tyler couldn't utter a word. His voice was frozen, so all he could do was nod and stare. Ethan grabbed Tyler's hand and brought to his chest, letting him feel every strong muscle in his body.

Not again! Tyler's hand froze. Time stopped, and he forgot how to breathe. This happened before. Not with Ethan, but with another boy once. The gym showers. Beau. A river of memories came flooding back to him and he left his spot on the bed.

He was back in high school, remembering his first kiss. He was sixteen, almost seventeen when it happened. He was a junior in high school and school was over for the day. Tyler had stayed behind. He couldn't remember what for. The hallways were empty, and the only sounds were that of a janitor mopping the floors. Tyler walked through the hallways with his books clutched tight to his chest, like a shield guarding his heart.

He walked past the school's pool and heard a splash. He peaked his head through and found Beau, the new student, swimming laps in the pool. Watching Beau swim was a thing of beauty. Like a dancer on stage, he was art in motion. For so long Tyler wondered what it would be like to kiss another boy on the lips. Sixteen and still in the closet, he never kissed anyone. Girl or boy. He would lie awake every night picturing a boy's soft lips, especially Ethan's.

The water grew still, and Tyler saw Beau treading water by the edge of the pool. His stare was intense. His bright green eyes were a deep jade. Tyler's cheeks grew red as the boy pulled himself out of the pool. His arms flexed and for Tyler it seemed to happen in slow motion. He remembered feeling like he was in a John Hughes movie and he was Molly Ringwald.

Beau stood on the hard tile floor, water dripping down his tan body. He ran a hand through his light brown hair, pushing it out of those intense eyes of his. Tyler couldn't stop his eyes from scanning Beau's body, watching the tiny drops of water cascade down his toned swimmer's body and over the bulge in the red speedo he wore.

"Beau, I am so sorry. I heard a noise and," but Tyler was cut off.

"Come on."

"What?"

Beau didn't say another word. He turned around and walked towards the locker room. Tyler raised an eyebrow and bit his bottom lip. Should he really be doing this? His palms grew wet with sweat, before his heart led him towards the locker room.

Steam filled the air like a heavy warm mist. The shower was running, and Tyler followed the sounds of running water. He put his books down on a bench and found Beau standing beneath the spray of hot water. The young swimmer watched Tyler with a smile on his lips. He ran his fingers down his muscles and hooked them onto the waistband of his swimsuit. He slowly pulled it down, teasing Tyler. The small barrier of fabric was all that separated Beau from Tyler's eyes. Tyler's breath caught in his throat and a small nervous smile developed upon his lips.

Beau slowly pushed the speedo down and Tyler needed to see more. The swimsuit fell to the boy's ankles, and Tyler's mouth fell open as he eyed his large flaccid penis. Tyler couldn't believe this was real. This stuff happened in his dreams, but not in real life.

He pinched himself on the arm, and he was awake.

Beau reached out for Tyler and grabbed his hand, pulling him beneath the water. The shower soaked through Tyler's clothes, but he didn't care the moment Beau's lips touched his. It was better than he ever dreamed. His lips were soft and full, and his tongue worked its way into Tyler's mouth. He guided his hands down his naked body letting him feel every last inch. That was when Tyler's life began and ended.

"What the fuck!"

Beau jumped away from Tyler, pushing him to the ground. Tyler turned around to find Chad and Todd, two of his high school bullies. They were rich, popular, and they were assholes. No one moved. All eyes were on him and Beau then. Tyler remembered how his lower lip quivered and how Beau stepped away from him.

"He fucking came at me in the showers! He tried to molest me, the faggot," Beau spit! His eyes were large and afraid, and tears ran down Tyler's face. He stood up and tried to run, but Chad had tripped him. Together with Todd, they beat the shit out of him. They punched him and kicked him repeatedly, leaving him on the ground. They would have left him to bleed to death, if they could. He went home that day with a black eye and a fractured rib. He lied to his father, telling him he fell down the stairs at school, but by the next day the whole school knew he was gay. Beau never looked his way again, except with disgust. And that was the story of Tyler's first kiss.

"Tyler," Ethan whispered, "you there?"

Ethan's voice brought Tyler back to the present and he looked up into Ethan's worried brown eyes. He pulled his hand away. Tyler blinked back the tears and looked away from Ethan, as he stood up.

"I'm sorry, I can't." Tyler ran out of the house, leaving

Ethan alone. Ethan watched from his window as Tyler pedaled away. What did Ethan do? He went too far. Damn it! What was wrong with him? How could he let his dick think for him? Tyler was fragile. He was delicate. Like a porcelain doll, if handled wrong he could crack. Ethan didn't want to crack him. He wanted to care for him. And he fucked up.

TYLER NEVER FELL ASLEEP that night. He stared up at the ceiling all night at the plastic glow-in-the-dark stars that he never took down. He knew they were silly, but sometimes he liked to wish upon them, and that night he wished for things to be okay. That was all he wanted, to be okay. Tyler grabbed the pendant he wore around his neck every day. It was a small amethyst crystal on a long brown leather cord. It fell down to the middle of his chest. Sometimes when life got hard, he would hold the pendant in his hand and think really hard. About what? Sometimes he didn't know. Whatever came into his. Any thought that would take his mind off whatever was going on his life.

Usually he'd think of Ethan, but what happened? He knew Ethan was nothing like Beau, but after the way Beau treated him in those gym showers and the way those guys outed him, how could he move on and be normal? Since that day, his life has been a living Hell. He let those assholes win again? Never did he report them? Who would have believed him over the popular students? And never did he recover from the trauma.

TYLER STILL LIED awake in bed as sun peaked through his window. He had to leave for work, but what was the point?

He would just disappoint Curtis once again, but the money always called to him. The thought of collecting enough cash, which he hid away from his father in the bottom of his closet stuffed into a shoe, to escape was more than enough reason to live through another day in Curtis's prison. Tyler dressed and went on his way. His father was out. He had to be at the construction site every morning at 5am. He liked to wake up early to have his time away from Hell.

As Tyler entered the hardware store, Nicole stood behind the register, ringing up one of the town hicks.

"Hey, Tyler. Curtis wants to see you in the back. Beware the viper's bite," she laughed, making two fangs with her index and middle finger, before swiping it through the air.

"Thanks for the warning, Nic."

Tyler clocked in and began his dreaded trek to the back-room. He silently shut the door and Curtis sat at the computer.

"Sit down, Tyler."

"Did I do something wrong, sir?"

"Just sit," his boss demanded. Tyler couldn't call Curtis abusive, but he could say his boss was a vile, malicious man.

Tyler sat down, but he didn't pull it closer to the older man. He folded his hands into his lap and looked down at the ground, biting his lip hard enough to taste the blood.

"Wuerth, do you know why I called you back here?"

Tyler shook his head. Curtis spun around in his chair and eyed the boy for the first time since he came into work. He smirked a rat-like smile. Tyler could feel nothing good was coming.

"Speak up!"

"No, sir."

"I can't hear you."

Tyler sighed. "I said, 'no sir.'" Tyler felt like he had joined the military and Curtis was the man leading the boot camp.

"Okay, Wuerth, I think it time for us to part ways." Curtis couldn't hold back his smile. He seemed to happy.

"What? Why?"

"I feel you don't work hard enough and after that woman's complaint I can't have an unstable worker."

Tyler clenched his fists. His knuckled turned white and they shook in his lap. *You fucking asshole!*

"Are you serious? I always bust my ass for you, Curtis. Everything you ask of me, I do. You know that woman was full of shit, you know it! Why don't you tell me what this is really about? You don't want a faggot ruining your reputation? Well fuck your business and fuck you!"

Tyler brought a hand to his mouth. Oh shit! I didn't just say that, did I?

Curtis stood up, towering over the boy. "Listen, you're gone. Get the hell out of my store, now!"

Tyler stood up and walked out of the backroom. Now what would he do?

"You okay?" she asked.

He gave her a weak smile, "I no longer work here."

"What! That is such bullshit! That asshole should be fired. He treats people like crap and you know what? He is a giant perv! I always see him checking out my ass."

Tyler laughed. "Thanks, but I'm going to head out. Take it easy, Nicole."

She gave him a hug before he left. He gave her a weak one back. He wasn't in the mood to be touched. Before she could say another word, he walked out. Nicole felt bad for Tyler. She didn't agree with the way the town treated him.

So, what if he was gay? The town treated him as if he went around killing puppies. He deserved much more than what he got.

Tyler found the wheels of his bike flat with a note left behind.

All the fucking time this happened! He couldn't take this anymore. Tyler fell to the ground and cried. What did he do to deserve all of this? He hated that job, but he needed it, so he could escape this town. He wanted to go to college and make something of his life. how would he get his tires fixed? Tyler opened the note:

Burn in hell faggot

He balled the note up in his fist and threw it to the ground. He would not cry this time. He had no more tears left in him to waste on this shit hole of a town. He began his long walk home, wheeling the bike along. It was a cloudy day and the air was dry. The sky looked gray and angry. Like a blink, lighting flashed, and a hard rain followed suit. Great! Tyler couldn't believe his great luck at that moment. After he was outed the whole world turned on him and he blamed one person for it. Beau was the reason his life was shit.

"Fuck you too!" Tyler barked at the sky.

A red pick-up truck pulled up alongside him and the window rolled down.

"Get in," Ethan spoke with that Southern drawl of his. Tyler just looked at him and began to cry. He was wrong about having no more tears. This town had a way of bringing out the pathetic in him. The rain soaked his shirt and mixed with his tears. Tyler felt thankful that Ethan couldn't see the tears from the rain, and he felt guilty about running away the night before.

Ethan stepped out of his truck and grabbed the bicycle

from his hands and threw it in the back. The rain soaked through his white tee shirt and it clung to his muscular chest, creating a second layer of skin. Tyler could make out every muscle beneath the shirt. Ethan helped the younger boy into his truck and turned the heat all the way up.

"Thanks," Tyler mumbled.

They drove off in silence. Nineteen long years of hell, he has been enduring and he didn't know how much more he could take. Each day took more and more out of him, and there wasn't much left of him.

Ethan pulled the car to the side of the road and slammed the steering wheel. Tyler jumped in his seat and apologized.

Ethan gave him a small smile. "I'm not mad at you. I'm just mad."

Tyler nodded. He was so disgusted. Too disgusted to even say a word. Disgusted with the people, this town, his life, and mostly himself. Tyler had always believed in God, but now he felt he was just a cruel player and Tyler was merely a pawn in a game of chess.

"It's not fair, Tyler. You're such a great person, but this town. Damn it! I hate this fucking town."

Tyler placed a hand on Ethan's shoulder. "Ethan, it's okay. I'm used to it."

Ethan turned towards him and looked right into Tyler's ocean-blue eyes.

"It's not okay. I can't stand to see you hurt like this. I," Ethan cut off. "I'm just so sorry. I wish I could do so much more."

TYLER'S TEARS came to an end and he wiped his cheeks clean. He looked up into Ethan's warm brown eyes and blushed.

"I am so sorry. I just soaked your tee shirt."

Ethan laughed. "Fuck the shirt. I'm sorry about last night. I shouldn't have done any of that. You were vulnerable and...Are you okay?"

"Yeah, thanks. It's fine. I just feel like a child. I am so embarrassed."

Tyler stared into Ethan's eyes, unable to look away. For years he had loved his best friend, wishing it would be requited, but also scared that it would be required. What if he lost his best friend? Since they were boys, they've always had one another. Each time his father beat him, Ethan saved him. After what Beau did to him in high school, Ethan was the one to comfort him and tell him everything would be okay. Ethan was his everything.

After the barn and last night, what were they now? Best friends, nothing, or more?

They sat in silence looking into one another's eyes. Their faces slowly grew closer, only inches away now. Was this really happening? It couldn't be, Tyler thought. It had to be his imagination, but when he felt Ethan's hard calloused hands on the sides of his face, he knew it wasn't. His fingers were warm as Tyler placed his hands on top of Ethan's. Closer they inched, and Tyler could almost taste Ethan's warm breathe. He closed his eyes and as he felt Ethan's lips on his own, the rest of the world melted away, and it was just the two boys. Tyler gripped onto Ethan's shirt, stretching the collar. Ethan moved his hands to Tyler's waist and pulled him closer to his body as he opened his mouth, his tongue meeting Tyler's. Neither one wanted to let go, afraid one of them would wake up only to learn it was all just a dream.

Ethan pulled away, but Tyler grabbed the back of his neck and pulled him back to his mouth. Their second kiss was hard. Teeth smashed, and they were clumsy. They grabbed at one another groping under their shirts, feeling each other's warm skin and their beating hearts.

Tyler felt happy, something he hadn't felt in a long time. Now if this was a dream, Tyler never wanted to wake up.

They parted again, and they looked at one another before breaking out into giggles. They turned to the radio realizing what song was playing. Heaven is a Place on Earth by Belinda Carlisle and Tyler couldn't agree with the lyrics any more than in that moment.

"Wow," Ethan muttered with a giant smile on his face. Ethan never expected that to happen. He just kissed his best friend.

"I've wanted this for so long," Tyler admitted. He backed away from Ethan and bit his bottom lip. He rubbed his sweaty palms together.

"I think I have too," Ethan answered, hugging Tyler close.

"Really?" Tyler wanted to believe this, but now he knew this was all impossible.

"Yes. I've never really truly known, but I always had a feeling I liked you. After the barn and then the other night, I should have called you, but I couldn't. Not yet. I had to think everything through. I didn't want to hurt you and I had to figure everything out. I've never been with a guy, you know? Girls yes, but I was never into any of the girls, but with you something clicked, and I can't imagine my life without you. You're not just my best friend, or my brother. You're so much more to me. I'm just sorry it took me so long to realize this."

Ethan placed a small kiss on Tyler's forehead. Tyler

smiled and sighed, closing his eyes. Ethan moved closer towards Tyler's slim frame and pulled him close.

"I've always hoped this would happen, but I was terrified of losing you. When did you realize you might be gay?"

Ethan shrugged his shoulders. "That's the thing, I still don't know what I am. Maybe I'm bisexual? Or pansexual, I think could be the term I'm looking for. But I'm sure of one thing. I want to be with you and no one else."

"Me too," Tyler whispered into Ethan's ear, before kissing his cheek.

Ethan drove with one hand and held Tyler's hand in the other. Ethan was still questioning everything, but in that moment, he knew he didn't need to question his love for Tyler. He really loved him.

As night fell, Ethan stopped the car on the side of the road and stepped outside. He grabbed Tyler by the waist and lifted him off the seat and brought him down to Earth. They still weren't sure if they were awake or not, but they were happy.

Ethan helped Tyler up onto the back of the truck. They looked up at the stars as they lied down. Tyler rested his head on Ethan's muscular chest and listed to the sounds of his heart. He didn't know what was going on or what they were to one another, but right now, Tyler didn't care. He was content.

Ethan woke up in his bed alone. Tyler went home last night after their cuddling beneath the stars. A weight was lifted off of his body. He was holding his breathe underwater for so long and now he finally surfaced and could breathe. He turned over to his side and looked out the window. The sun was shining, matching the way he felt. The gloomy day of yesterday was left behind.

Were he and Tyler together now? How exactly did this work out, he thought. How do you go from best friends to more? Tyler would no longer have to face this town alone. He was always there for him, but now they could truly face it together. Ethan really hoped he was ready for that. He envied Tyler. He was so brave to face the world. He could have lied and said it was a rumor, but he didn't He faced the world, and Ethan watched him struggle.

Could he tell his family? He knew his father would go crazy. But what about his mother and sister? He hoped they could accept them, he truly did, but doubt entered his mind. He dressed and walked outside to the stables. He smiled as he found Marshmallow, his favorite horse. She was all white with brown hair. She was beautiful. Ethan walked up to her and sat in her stall, picking up her brush. He brushed her side. He loved how she closed her eyes and enjoyed his touch. When he showed up, it was a spa day for her. They used to have a lot more animals but as his parents got older, it became too much to handle, so they sold most of the animals. Marshmallow was the only one to be kept. Ethan couldn't part from his girl.

He brushed his horse and let his mind clear. The cloudy mist dissipated, and everything was becoming clear. He wanted to be with Tyler. It was worth it. He would tell his parents. But not yet. He had to wait for the right time, at least that is what he was telling himself. Was he truly waiting or was he afraid his parents would react like Tyler's did? He couldn't be a coward. He had to be strong.

He kissed Marshmallow's nose and thanked her. Sometimes brushing her was all he needed to relax. He missed having the animals running around to care for. Being around them brought a joy to his life, that he felt was lacking from time to time. His mother always said he'd make a good veterinarian, but he didn't know if he'd be able to hand losing one on an operating table. He would love to have his own farm with his own animals, and maybe Tyler by his side. They could be like other happy couples. Married with children and animals. Why couldn't they have that?

He left the stables and jumped into his car. He had to see Tyler.

ERIN SAT in the station at her desk with a cup of coffee. She had a bad feeling in her stomach. David had been calling the station multiple times a day, but it's been two days of silence. He hasn't been outside handing fliers. No one in the station asked questions except for her. What happened to the doting father? Something was clawing at her insides. Something was wrong, and she didn't know what. She needed to know what exactly was going on. Her sister always said she had a sixth sense. Constance always believed Erin was a little psychic. It used to make Erin laugh, but she always knew when something bad was going to happen. She would get a feeling in the pit of her stomach, and it would continue to grow, planting roots all over her body until an intensifying worry took over her mind, shaking her to her core. It felt like a migraine for the entire body. But her feelings were just feelings, never anything more. No visions. No answers. Just an over-whelming emotion of worry and headaches.

Today she woke up with this feeling and knew it had to do with David. Something bad happened, or something bad was going to happen very soon. Cedar Creek was no longer going to be just a quiet town soon.

TYLER DIDN'T TELL his father he was fired. Why should he? It would be asking for another beating. He hoped his father would never find out. Tyler needed an escape from reality and without his father home, he took out one of his favorite records from the basket. A record of classic Judy Garland songs. These were his mother's records and the record player belonged to her as well. His father wanted to sell it, but Tyler begged him to keep it. When he played the music, not only did he disappear from this world, but he was also joined by his mother. Sometimes when he closed his eyes, he could feel the touch of her arms around him, singing into his ears.

The lush sounds blasted from the speakers and Tyler stood before full-body mirror. He sang to his reflection. He grabbed a scarf from his closet and a pair of sunglasses and danced around his room. He was Judy. His father hated his obsession with classic women like her, but Tyler looked up to them. Judy Garland, Barbra Streisand, Ella Fitzgerald, Nina Simone, Billie Holliday, and the list went on. These women inspired him and told him all would be okay.

He got his love from his mother. She too loved these classic female singers, and she passed her love of them down to him. Tyler thought back to the memories of them watching classic movies together on television. His mom would hold him in her arms and quote every line, and she never failed to tear up at the end. Even with comedies. She loved a good happy ending. Yet her life ended so sadly. It's funny how the world worked.

As a child, he would sneak into his parents' room and put on her heels and lipstick and stand in front of her mirror and pretend to be characters from movies, especially the Judy Garland ones. She was always his favorite movie star and to this day the actress still brought him hope. As he stood in front of his mother's mirrors wearing her shoes and make up, he'd quote the movies, like his mother did. His favorite scene to copy was the ending of A Star is Born. That final scene always killed him.

"Hello Everybody. My name is Mrs Norman Maine," he used to repeat.

The film was his mother's favorite, and over time it had become his favorite as well. He even had posters of Judy and Ella on his walls, along with pictures of Madonna and Cindy Lauper taped to his mirror. After his mother passed, he was forced to take it all down, and now nothing of his personality was left in his bedroom except for the childish glow-in-the-dark stars. His father told him only girls had rooms like his. Girls and fairies. Tyler cried all night, tearing apart his posters and pictures until nothing was left.

He hated his father.

The song finished, and Tyler was met with a heavy clapping. He spun around and found Ethan, his muscles filling out his tank top, leaning against the doorframe with a wide smile on his face. He hadn't shaved in a few days and the stubble was coming in strong, but still wasn't a beard yet.

"Bravo."

Tyler took off his scarf and sunglasses, putting them down on his bed.

"I didn't hear you come in."

"I snuck in."

"Creep."

Ethan smiled and walked up to the tall young man and pulled him down to kiss him. His height made Ethan feel like a dwarf, but he enjoyed it. He's never dated anyone taller than him, then again, he's never dated a man either. That is if they were dating.

"What are you doing here?"

"I was thinking we could go on a date. A real date, I mean."

Tyler couldn't help his smile. He nodded and followed Ethan out the door and to his truck. Ethan stopped the car outside the only movie theater in town and paid for two tickets. The theater was having a classic movie day, all day, and was showing West Side Story, that afternoon. Ethan hated musicals, and Tyler knew that. Tyler could have kissed him right there, if he wasn't so afraid. He couldn't let Ethan deal with what he did.

He didn't think about Ethan and his well-being. What

was this man getting himself into? Could Tyler truly let Ethan go through the agonizing torment every day like he did? Could he protect him?

They walked into the theater together and sat down side-by-side. A few people, mostly older men and women settled down into their seats.

"So West Side Story?"

"You love this movie," Ethan said with a bright smile.

"Yes, I do. But you hate it. What did you tell me? It's corny as Hell, I think was your exact quote."

"Maybe you could teach me to like it," he answered. Tyler liked the sound of that. He slightly nodded, and the lights came down. Together they watched as the gangs prepared to dance in the opening number. Tyler was wowed by their movement, but Ethan looked at Tyler. He watched his reactions. He studied the way his face reacting to the dancing, how he sang along to the songs, how he teared up at some scenes, and laughed at others. Their hands were only an inch apart. Ethan bit his lip as he slowly moved his fingers towards Tyler's. He glanced around, but no one could see them in the dark. All eyes were on the screen. All except his.

He took a deep breath and crawled his hand onto Tyler's, lacing his fingers through his. He saw Tyler tense up. He looked down at their hands and back up at Ethan. And smiled, with a small nod. This was okay, he was saying. Ethan quickly kissed his hand and smiled back. For the rest of the movie they sat like that, hand-in-hand, with Tyler watching the movie and Ethan watching Tyler.

When the lights came on, they detached their hands. Tyler missed the feeling of Ethan's fingers, like a child losing their parent in a store. They walked out of the theater in silence and out into the bright sun. Tyler wished it was night, so they could disappear together into the shadows. He wanted to be like anyone else and hold the man's hand and kiss him in public. But kissing Ethan wouldn't just mean the end of his life, but it would begin the destruction of Ethan's. His father was the sheriff for Christ's sake. If word got out the sheriff's son was a queer, Tyler was sure, he'd never see him again. He could see Sheriff Gardner shipping his grown son somewhere, just to keep him from turning into Tyler.

"Where to now?" Tyler asked.

"Neverland."

Tyler raised his eyebrows and looked over at Ethan, who began walking to his car. Tyler followed after. Neverland, that was a place he hadn't been to in a long time.

"Why now? We haven't been in almost a year."

"It's time to go back, Peter Pan," Ethan said with a childish delight. Sometimes Tyler would forget he was a twenty-year-old man.

Ethan first brought him to Neverland was about two years ago. It was a few days after he was outed. The school knew. The whole fucking town practically knew.

Worst of all, Ethan knew. Tyler didn't come back right away. He had to heal from his injuries, but on his first day back, Tyler walked through the school thinking Ethan must have hated him. He probably thought he was manipulating him to jerk off together. They slept in the same bed many times. Tyler couldn't face him. School started off bad, and only got worse. People laughed behind his back, while others called him names. By third period, his nightmare was only getting worse. Some of the students were starting to get physically abusive, and all the teachers turned a blind eye. Why should they stand up for the fag? He brought it upon himself, they thought.

For the first time he had ditched the rest of school that day.

Tyler left and ran to his bike, but Ethan had seen him running out of the school and chased him down.

"Tyler, wait!"

"Ethan, I'm so sorry. You must hate me. I am sorry I never told you I was...." He couldn't even say the word, it disgusted him so much. He was gay. Even thinking of it brought a burning bile to his throat.

"Shut up, Tyler! I don't hate you." He pulled the boy into a hug, not caring who saw. Fuck that kid, Beau and his asshole friends. "I still love you. You're my best friend, okay? Plus, I knew"

Tyler cried into his shoulder, nodding. Ethan knew?

Tyler wiped his tears away, and asked, "You Knew?"

Ethan smiled and wiped the tears off of his tee shirt. He started walking towards the parking lot. Tyler watched his back, wondering where he was going. Ethan turned around.

"Aren't you coming?"

Tyler had nodded and followed him to his car. The car ride was silent. The only sounds were of their breathing, and Tyler's light cries. He really hated crying. He felt so weak every time he did.

"Where are we going?"

"I'm taking you somewhere that helps me."

"Okay? You're not murdering me, are you?"

Ethan laughed. "If I wanted to kill you, you'd be dead by now."

"Funny."

Ethan laughed again. "Just hang on. We're almost there."

Tyler looked out the window. He wondered where Ethan was taking him. All he saw was trees and farms. The same as the rest of the town. Ethan parked the truck and helped Tyler out. He grabbed his backpack and followed Ethan onto a trail through the woods. If Ethan was trying to kill him, he was doing a horrible job trying to hide it. The only thing missing was a shovel for Tyler to dig his own grave. He heard so many stories of men coming out and their closest friends beating them and sometimes killing them.

The longer they trekked, Tyler grew irritable and demanded to know where they were going.

"We're almost there."

"You said that twice."

"Trust me, Tyler. I'd never do anything to hurt you." He looked back at Tyler and he knew Ethan was telling the truth. Tyler nodded and continued on until they left the woods and came to a clearing.

"Wow."

Before Tyler, they stood at the most beautiful lake. It was a large lake shaped like an egg. Trees surrounded it on all sides, with a small shack nearby. The sky was blue, Tyler remembered. Barely a cloud and the sun shone bright, dancing on the lake like twinkling stars.

"This is Neverland," Ethan said.

"It's beautiful," he responded.

And now here they were again. Tyler almost forgot how lovely it was. He stood beside Ethan, who held his hand.

"I missed this place," Ethan spoke. "I used to come here whenever things got hard. I know it sounds cowardly, but sometimes I just had to get away."

"It's not. We all need to escape somewhere. You have Neverland, and I had you." Tyler's cheeks grew hot as he admitted Ethan was his escape. Ethan didn't seem to mind as he pulled the boy closer to his body and wrapped his muscular arms around him.

"Let's go swimming."

"I didn't bring a suit," Tyler uttered.

Ethan let go of him and licked his lips. He slowly pulled his shirt up, taking his time, making sure his stomach muscles tensed as he threw his shirt off. He was doing it on purpose to tease Tyler. Tyler could tell. With a smile, Ethan pulled down his pants and kicked off his shoes. He stood before Tyler in only his briefs. A tiny red pair. He ran for the lake and dived in. Tyler laughed, pulling off his clothes, until he was also in his briefs. He ran after and dived into the water.

Together and alone, they found their wish to becoming true.

In the water they swam and laughed, having fun. Everything disappeared. Nothing could harm them in Neverland. They were the only humans left on the Earth now, and nothing could stop them. Ethan pulled him close and kissed him, holding Tyler in the water, his arms wrapped around his waist.

In the shed, Tyler was amazed how beautiful it looked. Ethan fixed up the inside. What was once a crumbling box in ruins, now was a small home. Inside were lights, a bed, and a rug. Ethan lied down on the bed and pulled Tyler down with him.

"I want you to come here whenever you need to get away from anything."

"How do I get here?"

"I got you covered." Ethan reached over into a small nightstand and opened the drawer. He pulled out a silver skeleton key and a map. "I made a copy of my key. This key will get you inside here, and this map will tell you how to get the lake from the town."

Tyler pulled him into a kiss.

"Thank you. Thank you so much." Tyler no longer cared about his father or the town. His past didn't matter.

CHAPTER

TEN

Tyler sat up in bed and looked over at Ethan, who lightly snored. He had kicked the blanket off of his almost nude body in the night. His small briefs left little to Tyler's imagination. Tyler watched his chest inflate with each breath. Tyler lied down on his side and watched him sleep. He ran his fingers down his muscular chest, letting the stubble of tiny hairs tickle his skin. He placed a small kiss on his nipple, feeling it grow hard in his mouth.

"That feels good."

Tyler smiled, "Did I wake you?"

"No. I wasn't asleep."

"Liar. You were snoring."

"I don't snore."

Tyler looked around the small shed-apartment.

"I still can't believe what you did here."

"Yeah. Last time you were here it was a shitty little shack. I wanted to turn it into a small home of sorts. There's no bathroom or anything, but I was able to get the other things that matter. Electricity, a bed. It's like a secret place no one knows of except me. My Neverland."

He pulled Tyler close and kissed his forehead.

"Our Neverland."

Ethan's cheesy romantic side used to bother Tyler, but now that the sentiments were for him, he loved them. He rolled on top of Ethan and kissed him. All worries evaporated like the morning dew.

The day wore on and it was time to part. Tyler couldn't stand to leave Ethan or Neverland, but it was time for reality to bare its ugly little head. Why must that always happen? When a dream was at its best, it was time to wake up. In silence they walked hand-in-hand to his car and listened to the one radio station the town had. All country music and oldies. Ethan liked the station, but he always loved country music. He really was a cowboy, Tyler thought.

Tyler entered his house and found himself back on his bed. Alone, once more. Now that he knew the feeling of Ethan's arms, he wished to be back in them.

Ethan drove into town, parking outside the hardware store. He walked inside, ripping the doors open and looked around. Where was the dumb son of a bitch? He found Curtis in the store, and Ethan had to do everything in his power from knocking his hillbilly lights out.

"How can I help you today, Ethan?"

"By burning in Hell, you homophobic piece of shit. I know how you treated Tyler. You won't' get away with it. My daddy is the sheriff, and I will make sure he knows what kind of business you run here."

Curtis narrowed his eyes and poked the young man in the chest.

"Listen here. I run this place the way I want. You don't

walk in all high and mighty and act all tough. I fired Tyler, and good riddance. Why do you care? Are you faggot too?"

Nicole turned the corner into the aisle to see Ethan punch her boss in the nose. The asshole went to the ground, clutching his nose as blood poured down his face. Ethan rubbed his knuckles and looked down at the ugly fuck.

"Next time, you won't be so lucky."

"You crazy asshole! I can sue you for that."

"Not if you touched me first."

"How do you plan to prove that?"

Ethan smiled and licked his dry lips. "Well I have a witness right here."

Curtis laughed. "You think she will help you?"

Nicole walked up to Ethan and placed a hand on his shoulder. She stared down at the pathetic excuse of a man and smiled. He was where he belonged, on the floor with the dirt.

"I don't know. I did see you touch him, so by law you harassed him first, sir."

"Get out of here, Gardner. Now."

"With pleasure!" Ethan smiled and sauntered off, proud of himself. He wasn't really going to tell his father, but it was damn good to scare a shithole like Curtis. Hopefully next time he'll think twice about how he treats his workers.

And how to treat Tyler. Ethan walked towards the street, running across. The air was growing hotter as June was coming to an end. The air was heavy with heat and sweat. Ethan was feeling the sweat drip down his back, beneath his plaid shirt. He unbuttoned a few more buttons up top, expose more of his chest and torso. Rolling up his sleeves, he looked into the window of Vera's Room. In the window sat a stuffed dog, a rather adorable one that looked like it could have been a basset hound. Ethan smiled, remembering the basset hound he had as a child. The dog grew up with him but died nearly four years ago. His name was Bailey, and he loved the dog. It wasn't just a pet, but it was his family. Ethan didn't understand how people disliked animals. He didn't trust anyone who could dislike an animal.

Ethan entered the shop and took the stuffed dog from the window and paid for it.

The owner of the shop was Vera Hawkins, a sweet elderly woman who lived alone on the edge of town. She smiled at Ethan as she took his money.

"Lovely day we are having?"

"Yes, ma'am. How are you, Miss Vera?"

She gave him a wide smile. "I'm just swell. I've told you many times. It's just Vera."

"You'll always be Miss Vera to me, Miss Vera."

She laughed and bid him a good day. She was always so charming, brining lightness to a town that lacked compassion. She might have been the beating heart behind Cedar Creek.

As he walked to his car, he hugged it tight. The fabric was soft, like velvet, but fluffier like a cotton ball. The belly was fat and overstuffed, perfect for cuddling at night. The ears were brown and hung low and it had a pair of sad eyes. As Ethan hugged the stuffed animal tighter, the dog began to whimper, catching the man by surprise. He burst out into laughter, taking in the stuffed friend.

NIGHT FELL, and Tyler snuck onto the roof and lied down. He looked up at the stars, which shined so bright. He closed his eyes and brought a finger to his lips. Ethan's kiss lingered upon his lips. He still couldn't believe he and Ethan have been kissing, and becoming more than friends, he thought. The first kiss was magical. Sloppy, hard, yet perfect. Within that dark red truck as the rain pattered the roof, creating the perfect soundtrack to kiss by. And the song on the radio. Heaven is a Place on Earth. He needed to hear it again. The song played on repeat in his head and he desperately wanted to hear their song. Was it their song? He always heard about couples having songs and possibly that could be theirs.

Tyler closed his eyes and felt the wind chill his body. After the hot day, it felt good on his skin. He zipped up his hoodie and placed his hands behind his head. The kissing has been wonderful, and the time they shared in the barn was heaven itself, but what if Ethan wanted to go farther. Would he be ready? He knows Ethan had slept with girls, but what if Tyler disappointed him in bed. The last time he had been with someone...it was a nightmare he would never want to relive. No one knew of what happened, not even Ethan, and he hid nothing from his best friend. And then there was the other night where he freaked with his best friend. What was wrong with him?

He opened his eyes and sat up to welcome the world. Reality was crashing down. He wanted to make love with Ethan. He's thought about it many times, but could he truly give all of himself to him, even the man he's loved for so long?

It was all because of Beau. Everything fucked up with his life stemmed back from that classmate of his. He wished the boy would disappear from the town. He didn't wish death on him, or at least he didn't want to, but sometimes that was all he wished on him.

He really did scare himself sometimes. Wishing death on people? Freaking out on Curtis, even though he deserved it. There was a wild animal caged within him, and what would happen when it was released? Would anyone who stood in his path survive, or would all be destroyed?

He knew he was being silly, but sometimes his neurotic mind controlled his every move. He had to get back inside. The wind no longer felt comforting. The blanket had turned into a bed of nails and the wind was biting him. No longer caressing.

He closed the window as he stepped onto his bed. He needed to ease his mind. He went to his basket of records and pulled out the one to always cheer him up. The Wizard of Oz. He placed the record on and played it loud. He closed his door. His father was not home. Probably passed out in the bar again, but Tyler didn't fucking care. He had no love for his father. That's what he told himself. He would never admit it, but somewhere he still cared. Only the stars would know why, but he did.

As his favorite song came on, "Over the Rainbow," Tyler drifted off into his imagination, imagining himself on Dorothy's farm singing to the skies. He too wished to belong somewhere else. Somewhere beautiful.

Somewhere he could be loved.

He sang the lyrics, his tender voice mixing with the bravado of Judy's. A delicate mix, but it worked. It had gotten his mother's voice. He had her blue eyes and her blonde hair. Every day he was thankful he looked exactly like her, and nothing like this father.

OFF IN THE grist mill was the Miller. He sat on the ground, his back to the wall. He sat between the bodies of Talia and Lucas. The old man lied on his side across the room. Rabbit-face didn't want to play with the man. He was too old, and the Miller was hungry. He bit into the carcass of a rat and tore off its flesh with his disgusting rotting teeth. He dug into the little belly and ripped out the organs of the tiny rodent and held it up to each one of their mouths. The Miller growled and forced the bloody little organs into each of his victim's mouths. He jumped up and smelled their rotting flesh. The Miller barked and hopped around his friends. He fell onto Talia's lap and lied his head back on Lucas's crotch. The Miller closed his eyes and spoke to his friends in yips and barks.

The door opened, and a woman stepped inside.

"Hello," she called out.

The Miller stood up, sniffed the air. She had the smell of an old room, wet with mildew and left to dry. It mixed with her perfume. It was a potent blend of baby powder and lilacs. The Miller took his bloody sickle in hand and walked towards the woman.

ELEVEN

Tyler wandered through the record shop, peaking through each and every stack. He needed to be out of the house. His father didn't have work that day and he was passed out in his bedroom. The boy couldn't be there when the drunk decided to wake up. With a pounding headache, he might choose to take it out by pounding Tyler. He had enough saved up money hidden, that he was able to take some money out. He would treat himself to a new record, but he was looking for a certain one. The shop had any record possible, so he knew it was here. It just a matter of time until he found it.

"B-E, B-E, B-E," he repeated beneath his breathe.

"Can I help you with something?"

Tyler looked up to find the owner, Gerald Lamp peering at him from over his glasses. He was a gentle old man. Frail and covered in wrinkles and age spots.

"Yeah, I'm looking for Belinda Carlisle," Tyler answered.

The old man stood up and grabbed his cane. What should have been a small walk, was a large trek for him. Just taking one step was like climbing Everest for him. With each step, his body shook, and Tyler felt bad. He could have found the album himself, but the man was by his side, going through the bins, until he pulled out her records.

"Here you go."

"Thank you so much!"

Tyler took all the records and went through all of them, reading the track listing. Once he found the one with the song from their first kiss, he grabbed it and paid. He clutched the record to his chest like a newborn babe. He couldn't wait to hear the song again and imagine their first kiss.

TYLER ENTERED his house and hummed beneath his breathe as he walked to his bedroom. He had to stop himself from racing up the stairs. He didn't want to wake his father. He planned to connect his headphones and lie in bed. He walked to the top of the stairs and found his door wide open. He never left it open. As he walked towards his bedroom, his heart took a nosedive into the pit of his stomach. He felt like he was going to choke on his own organ.

"No," he cried out as he looked into his bedroom. His room was torn apart, and his father sat on his bed. His clothes were thrown everywhere, and the record player had been destroyed. His records were broken in half.

"Why?"

His father stood up and glared right into his boy's eyes, anger flashing before them.

"You're pathetic. A pathetic faggot. I know what goes on in this room of yours. Bringing boys to your room. Letting them touch you. Letting them fuck you. Filthy piece of shit. You're lucky I let you live underneath this roof. You're not going anywhere," he slurred.

What did he mean? He couldn't have found it.

Tyler dived for his closet and dug through the clothing and the shoes. The money. All the money he had saved up was gone.

"Looking for this?"

Tyler looked around and found Frank holding a wad of cash. His cash. He couldn't do this. He made that money. It was his. Not this man pretending to be his father. His father died years ago, along with his mother.

"You can't take that. It's mine. I made that money!"

Frank laughed, grabbing a bottle of whiskey from the floor. Always drunk. Always fucking drunk. The bastard.

He shoved the money into his pants and laughed. Even his laughter was disgusting. More of a choking than a laughing.

"You have to give me that back. Please, I'm begging you, Dad!"

He reached up to grab the money from the man's pocket, but Frank stepped back and punched Tyler across the face. Tyler fell to the ground and curled up into a ball as the monster beat him and kicked him. He continued to cry until the beating was over and his father was gone. His body ached, and his bones felt brittle.

He tried to sit up and looked around. The record player was smashed. His mother's record player. The one that had comforted him over all these years. The records destroyed, all except for the one he bought that day. Everything hurt, but most of all his heart felt like it was being stabbed by a million knives at once over and over again. His mother died for a second time in his life. He grabbed the photograph of her, pulling it out of the broken frame and held it close to his chest and cried.

He hated his father.

. . .

ERIN KNOCKED on David's door. She rang the doorbell twice and called thrice that day. *Where has this man been?* She grabbed the handle finding the door unlocked. He really was losing it. She entered the house and pulled out her gun as she searched through the house. She knew David. He was always a neat professional man, but the house was in disarray and he was nowhere. Like his daughter he disappeared.

Her gut feeling grew worse each hour of each day. The longer he was gone, the more she knew she was right. Something bad was going on in Cedar Creek. Something really bad.

ETHAN WATCHED a movie with his young sister on the couch when the doorbell rang. Who could that be, he wondered. He was happy for the distraction as well. He loved his sister dearly, but the movie she was making him watch was God awful. But Gracie loved it, and he would do anything to make his girl happy.

His mother answered the door.

"Ethan, come here."

Ethan stood up and walked towards the door, wondering who was calling for him. He stopped at the sight of a bloody, battered Tyler, tears running down his face.

"What? Tyler!"

He ran to him and pulled him into a tight hug. Tyler cried onto his shoulder. Grace entered the foyer.

"Mommy, what's wrong with Tyler?"

"Grace, go up to bed."

"But..."

"Please, Grace. I will tuck you in soon."

Grace nodded and ran up the stairs. Cynthia closed the door and led the boys to the kitchen. They sat down at the kitchen table, while Ethan's mother wet a towel in the sink. She didn't speak as she cleaned the blood up from his face.

"Tyler, this has gone long enough. You should stay here for a few days, until we figure everything out. I cannot allow you to live with that man any longer."

"But, he's my...father." Even the word disgusted him. Frank. He was no father. He was something despicable. He was a nightmare come to life. He was Dracula to Tyler's Mina. He was sucking his life away each and every day, until nothing would be left except for a hollow shell of a human.

Cynthia sighed. "Honey, he really isn't. Michael is working late tonight. I think we should talk to him."

"Please don't. I don't want to make this a big deal."

"Tyler, why?" Ethan asked. He grabbed his friend's hand. Cynthia looked at their hands, fingers intertwined. They looked into one another eyes in a way she and Michael used to. She smiled, happy for her son. She always wanted him to meet the right person, and while she wished it was a woman, she was happy it was Tyler. The boy was a second son to her. She watched him grow up and he's slept over most nights. If Ethan was happy, she was happy.

Ethan looked up, catching his mother's eye. He pulled his hand away, but she grabbed his hand and placed it back in Tyler's. The boys smiled at the older woman. Ethan had never thought his mother was as beautiful as she was in that very moment. Her smile was small, possibly sad, but also genuine. Ethan could read the love in her eyes, and he loved her too.

"I won't tell your father, okay."

Ethan nodded. Tyler threw his arms around her. She rubbed his back and smiled. She loved the boy. She honestly did. What the town did to him wasn't right. He was the same boy. He loved differently than others, but he loved, and he deserved love.

"Now get some sleep, and we will discuss everything tomorrow."

Ethan kissed his mother's cheek and pulled Tyler up to his room. They undressed down to their underwear and crawled beneath the covers of his bed. Tyler lightly sobbed. Ethan wrapped his arms around his waist and pulled him in closely. He wished he could do more. Fuck! He felt helpless watching the man he loved disappear. All he wanted to do was take his pain away.

"Have you ever thought about running away?"

"What?" Tyler turned around and looked right into his lover's eyes. "Run away?"

"Yes. Get away from here. Away from this town. We can start a new life."

Tyler smiled and shook his head. "That's not realistic."

Ethan nodded and held him tight as Tyler fell asleep. He didn't sleep. He couldn't sleep. He had to protect him. Make sure nothing bad happened. He would take on the role of protector. He kissed the back of Tyler's head, breathing in the scent of his shampoo.

Tyler slept, and he dreamed. He dreamed of the town's cruelty and the incident in the gym showers all those years ago. He dreamed of his father. He dreamed of what his father could do to him. In his dream he never left. He got old and died in the town, only for it to end with his father tearing him apart.

He woke up screaming in the bed, sweating. Ethan sat

up and held him close. He shushed him and rubbed his back.

"It's okay. Tyler, it's okay. I'm here. Shush, I'm here."

Tyler nodded and cuddled into Ethan's body, nuzzling his face into Ethan's neck. Ethan held him as close as he could. No one would know where one person began and the other ended. Their legs were tangled, and their bare skin touched. Everywhere they felt warm and Tyler felt safe. As Tyler fell back to sleep, Ethan stayed up rubbing his head. Ethan thought back to their kiss they had only recently shared. He studied Tyler's innocent pale face. He slept like a child. He was peaceful. Beautiful.

Angelic.

As he watched Tyler sleep, he caressed the soft skin of his cheek and in that moment, Ethan knew he was in love with Tyler. He's always loved him, but he was in love with Tyler. His best friend and lover.

Lover.

Such a funny word. To call someone a lover, especially when they've been best friends all their lives. Yet it didn't seem strong enough a word to call Tyler. Was he his lover? Maybe there wasn't a word to describe how Ethan felt for Tyler. Possibly their love defied the power of language.

TWELVE

The sun broke through Ethan's window. Tyler woke up to Ethan's soft fingers tracing down the spine of his back. Tyler smiled and let out a soft moan.

"That feels good," he whispered, melting into Ethan's touch like honey.

"Good." He ran his hands down Tyler's sides. "I want you to feel good."

Tyler turned around and kissed him. He rolled over on top of him and hugged him close.

"I wish we could stay like this all day," he admitted.

"We could. Mom and Grace are going to see my aunt today and Dad left for the station already. We could go to Neverland. That is if you're not bored of me yet."

"I would never get bored of you."

As they swam and laughed, they forgot their worries. When the sun was at its hottest, Tyler and Ethan were lying on the grass staring up at the clouds above them. They watched them move, taking in all of their shapes. Ethan had his hands behind his head, while Tyler had his clasped on his chest.

"Tell me a story."

Tyler looked over at Ethan, whose eyes were closed. He had a look of content, as if nothing could ever harm him.

"A story?"

"Yeah, just like the ones you used to tell me as a boy."

A story. What kind of story, Tyler wondered. He hadn't made up a story in years. He didn't have any stories to tell. Adulthood had a way of killing a person's imagination.

"Um," Tyler began. "There was once a small boy. He lived in a village far away. It was a small village, the kind where everyone got along. They all respected each other, well except for the boy. He wasn't like any of the other villagers. He was different. Odd, I guess. He kept his secrets hidden and the town thought him a mystery, and *that* the town feared."

The words flowed like a waterfall. His imagination slowly came back to him. He opened the door and now they were racing through the entrance. The words came to him as the story appeared in his mind like a movie playing for only him.

Ethan turned to his side and opened his eyes, resting his head in his palm.

"Go on."

Tyler took a deep breathe, "The boy had no friends. He had his mother, but she died many years ago. It was only him and his father now. The boy's father told him he loved him, and he became his son's only friend.

"But one night the boy was hungry, and they had no food. They were starving, so his father decided to leave their cottage and get dinner for them. His father was gone for hours and the boy grew worried. The clock struck midnight, and his father returned, carrying a single red apple. It was red like the autumn leaves outside and when the boy took that first juicy bite, he swore it was the most delicious thing he had ever tasted.

"But the boy would go on to regret eating the apple. He realized the man who stood there wasn't his father. He looked like his father, but this man was cruel. He was..." Tyler stopped and took a deep breath. His face was wet, and he felt a sob stuck in his throat.

"Tyler, you don't have to go on."

Tyler ignored his best friend and continued on with the story. Now that he began, he had to finish it. Something inside him was screaming to be heard. Ethan once called Tyler a "Weaver of Words."

"The boy grew withdrawn." Tyler wiped away his tears. "Each day his father asked more of his son. At first it was simple requests, but the boy's father was also hungry. It wasn't so bad at first. All he wanted was fruit. The boy would go out, pick the juiciest red apples he could find, and bring them back to the man pretending to be his father. The boy wanted to leave but he was afraid. He didn't want to believe it, but in his heart, he knew his actual father was dead.

"The man's appetite grew, and the stranger began to crave meat. The boy never hunted before, but the man forced the boy to kill the animals himself. The boy had trouble, but he knew that if he didn't, he wouldn't be alive for much longer. The thought of death kept him going. When the meat of the animals no longer satiated his appetite, the man was hungry for only just one thing. The flesh of a child. Particularly the boy."

Ethan bit his lip, wishing he could do something to help his best friend. He lightly touched his soft hand.

"The boy had no clue what to do. He tried to run, but no one in the village heard his cries. When the sun rose on the sleepy little town, the boy was no more, and the man had disappeared."

Tyler could no longer hold back his tears. They stained his cheeks. Ethan sat up and pulled Tyler to his chest, hugging him tight. Tyler sobbed into Ethan's neck and Ethan rubbed circles beneath Tyler's shirt on his back.

"It's okay. I'm here, Tyler. I'm here. Nothing can harm you while I am here. Nothing, I promise." Ethan breathed in Tyler's smell and felt a wave in his chest. No, his heart. All he wanted to do was hold Tyler and kiss him. He wanted him to know he'd be safe with him.

They held one another in silence and when the wind grew cold, they got dressed and drove back to Ethan's house. Mrs Gardner was cooking dinner in the kitchen, and Grace was coloring on the floor. Ethan and Tyler went up to his bedroom and lied on the bed together. Tyler fell asleep in his arms and Ethan lied there holding him. Even when his arm fell asleep, he didn't move it. Tyler needed to rest. He would think of something. He and his mother would find a way to get Tyler out of that house. He thought about letting him live in the shed, but with no bathroom or running water, it'd be impossible. Then there is their house, but would his father go for the idea?

He only knew one thing and that was he had to protect Tyler.

Grace knocked on the door letting them know dinner was ready. Ethan woke Tyler up and together they walked downstairs. As they all sat down, Sheriff Gardner walked through the door. He took off his holster and jacket and sat down at the table.

Michael wasn't comfortable with Tyler staying over. He didn't know how he let Cynthia talk him into it. Yeah, the boy had issues, but it was between him and his father. The kid brought it upon himself. He chose to be gay.

Cynthia looked up at her husband, shaking her head. She has never been so ashamed of him in her life. He didn't look at Tyler like a person. He looked at him like a wild animal that needed to be put down. So much disdain in those dark eyes of his. It saddened her.

Ethan noticed his father's look as well, as did Tyler. Tyler tried to ignore it, but he looked at him the same way his own father did. His eyes told him everything. Sheriff Gardner thought he was revolting. He was a cockroach that wouldn't leave their home. He couldn't wait to be done with dinner and as they finished, he and Ethan went back upstairs.

"I'm sorry," Ethan apologized.

"About what?"

"My father and the way he treated you."

"He didn't say anything," Tyler answered but he knew what he meant.

"That's the point. He ignored you the entire night. It was horrible."

Ethan hugged him and lied down on the bed with him. They held one another and faced each other. Their legs were tangled and their faces only inches apart. Ethan got rid of the space and kissed him. It wasn't passionate. It was a soft kiss. A loving kiss. The kind of kiss that told a person they were safe, and everything was okay.

As the young men kissed, Tyler thought back to the day he was outed. He didn't want to, but the memories continued to swarm him. They were a horde of wasps stinging him everywhere. It was the day after Ethan first took him to Neverland. School had been horrible, and his father had gotten word of what happened. His father had begun beating him. The beatings grew worse and then one day at school the bullying took an extreme new course. Tyler remembered screaming that day, but no one had heard him. Or no one cared. Who'd come to his rescue? The school would let the faggot die. When he got home, he was defeated. He was too tired to stand. He was too tired to face his father. Too tired to make it to the next day. Too tired to live.

He remembered stripping off his clothes and turning on the water in the bath. He sat in the bathtub, the water burning his skin red. At that moment in life, Tyler felt worthless. He dreaded what the next day would bring. He remembered how he pulled his knees up to his chest and wrapped his arms around his legs. He dunked his head into the water and screamed. He screamed loud and hard. He screamed until there was nothing left except for the water filling his mouth. He thought about keeping his face beneath the water and letting himself drown. He'd never see the next day or worry about what would happen.

But then he thought of Ethan. His beautiful, kind best friend, Ethan. He couldn't leave him alone like that. Being best friends, he had made a promise to him, and by dying, he'd go back on it. He pulled his head out of the water.

He opened the drain and let the water fall in like a whirlpool. He stepped out of the bathtub and wrapped a towel around his slim waist. He wanted to delay going to sleep. If he fell asleep, he would have to be in school again much sooner to deal with the rest of those jerks.

He settled in bed. He took his glasses off and placed

them on the nightstand, before turning out the light. He used to pray before bed, but as he got older and learned just how cruel the world was, he stopped. If God didn't care about him, why should he care about God?

What if something happened again? And if it did with Ethan, he'd have no one and nothing to save him this time. Ethan was the reason why he decided to survive onto the next day.

And the next day was bad. He thought about calling out sick, but his father was already drunk and in a bad mood. When Tyler arrived at school, he wandered through the hallways like a ghost. He didn't want to be seen. He had wished he was dead. The secret he had kept for so long, the one he tried to keep from himself.

"Ethan?"

"Yeah?"

"Do you remember that night I tried to kill myself."

Ethan's eyebrows scrunched and his lip slightly quivered. He nodded. He didn't want to remember that night. Was Tyler thinking about trying it again?

"There is something I never told you."

"What? You can tell me anything."

Tyler took a deep breath and looked into those warm brown eyes he loved so much and finally said the secret which haunted him for so many years.

"The shower incident wasn't the only time. After I healed up and went back to school, it was gym class. I waited until all the other guys went home before I took my shower. We were swimming that day. One of the guys, a football star, stayed behind though." Tyler took a deep breath. "He grabbed me from behind. He grabbed me by the neck and he held me against the wall. He was choking me. I couldn't breathe. I couldn't fight back. I honestly thought I was going to die."

"Oh Tyler."

"He let go and threw me to the floor. I crashed so hard. He grabbed my legs and spread them open. Ethan, I was naked. He spread my legs open and undid his pants. He told me 'all fags deserved this,' and he…" Tyler had never said it out loud. He had to. He needed to.

"He raped me."

THIRTEEN

Kaitlyn had stayed in the motel longer than she expected. One night turned into four nights. The rest was doing her good and now she was ready to leave. What would she see next, she questioned. She's seen so much in her trip across the country and has documented nearly everything. Most people would find her photographs boring, but she found the rural life out here so fascinating. The farms, the animals, the people. Everything seemed so clear. Even the air felt clearer. She never how air could feel different, but now that she has been to places far away from the city life she knew, she didn't know if she could go back to that kind of heavy air.

She missed the busy life. While it's been nice to pause for a while, she desired to hit play on her life again.

She sat on the hard motel mattress, packing away her clothes. Her camera sat around her neck. She wanted to get a few more photos of the motel before leaving. Even the attendant posed for a photograph. He truly ended up being a sweetheart. He was as far removed from Norman Bates as one could get.

When she checked out, he was sad to see her go. He felt that he made a friend and enjoyed having her stay at the motel the past few days. He gave her a discount on the room, charging her only for two nights instead of the four.

"I can't accept that," she said.

"Yes, you will. Thank you for keeping me company."

Kaitlyn smiled and lifted up her camera.

"Let's take a picture together."

He smiled brightly, and Kaitlyn aimed the camera so both she and her new friend could be in the picture together. He helped her bring her bags to the car and as she drove off, his smile fell from his face and once again he was alone.

Ethan couldn't believe what Tyler told him the night before. Ethan had woken up, but last night was still heavy in the air. Tyler slept beside him. Ethan watched his chest inflate. Tyler deserved to sleep.

Last night, as Tyler told him, Ethan sat up in the bed. "What?" How did he never know? He should have known. "Tyler, look at me. Please."

Tyler had stared at the wall in front of him. No tears fell from his eyes. He sat there with his knees up to his chin and his arms wrapped around his long thin legs. He wouldn't look at Ethan. No matter what Ethan said, Tyler wouldn't dare move his eyes in his direction. Even as they lied down in bed, Tyler fell asleep facing the wall. He wouldn't let Ethan hold him or touch him.

Ethan stepped off the bed and pulled on jeans and a flannel. He found his mother in the kitchen making coffee for herself. It's been a long night for everyone, he guessed.

Cynthia grabbed his shoulder and handed him the mug of coffee. He smiled at her and thanked her.

Tyler opened his eyes. He'd been awake but couldn't bring himself to look at Ethan. How could he? Ethan wouldn't want to be with him anymore, now that he knew he was a used-up slut. He never knew why he blamed himself, but he did. He hated how he did. He tried to pretend the memory didn't exist. If he didn't think about it, then it never happened.

Bullshit!

Every time he flashbacked to the rape, the feelings of self-hatred and disgust swarmed back as well. He could hear Ethan and Mrs Gardner talking downstairs. He couldn't quite make out the words. He sat up in bed and reached over for his skinny jeans. His father always called them girl jeans. Tyler buttoned up last night's shirt and laced up his boots. He walked downstairs into the kitchen.

"Good morning, Sweetie," Mrs Gardner greeted him. Tyler gave her a weak smile in return. "Sit down. I'm gonna make breakfast soon."

"That's okay. I've taken up too much of your time. Thank you so much for everything, but I should go home."

"Tyler?"

"Thank you, so much."

Tyler left the house and walked away. In the kitchen Cynthia looked at Ethan, her eyebrows raised.

"What happened?"

"I'm not too sure."

Ethan stood up and ran out of the house. Tyler didn't get down the road too far without his bike. Ethan called out his name, but Tyler kept on walking. Ethan caught up and grabbed his shoulder.

"Tyler, where are you going?"

"I told you, I'm going home."

"But why? You know it's not safe there for you."

"You don't deserve me, Ethan. I opened up to you and now you know the truth. I feel disgusting."

"What happened to you was not your fault! Don't you know that?"

"I know, but I don't know. I can't think right now. My mind is a fog and my words are jumbled. I'm lost, and I can't find my way back. I hear you calling my name, but the fog is so heavy that your voice sounds low and I can't find you."

Ethan grabbed his hands and kissed him. "Listen to my voice. I'm here. I'm not going anywhere."

Tyler closed his eyes and nodded. A lone tear escaped an eye and Ethan kissed the tear, letting it slip between his lips. Ethan pulled him back towards his home. He refused to let Tyler go back to that house. Frank hadn't even called to check up on his son. If anyone was disgusting it was Tyler's so-called father.

Cynthia was happy to see the boys come back. They sat down at the table and silently held hands. She smiled at the way they looked at one another. True love, she thought. She wanted to Tyler to feel safe. He has gotten quite skinny recently, not to the point of looking anorexic, but at the rate he was going in that house, he would be there soon.

She decided to make French toast for the boys. She's never been so proud of her son. He was showing himself to be a strong young man. Compassionate, loving, and selfless. Exactly the way she wanted him to be. She sat down and ate and watched as Tyler inhaled the food. He nearly choked forgetting to chew. Ethan rubbed his back and ate.

After breakfast they offered to clean, but she laughed them off and told them to relax. They went back upstairs, and she took care of the dishes. She had to think of something to help Tyler. She felt like she was running out of time. She didn't know why but there seemed to be a time-bomb counting down, and it would only lead to destruction.

ETHAN AND TYLER lied in the barn, their shirts missing. Ethan held the blonde close to his body. He didn't care how hot it was inside the barn. He wanted to be as close to Tyler as he could.

"I've got a gift for you," Ethan said.

"You do?"

"It's back in my bedroom."

The two young men lied in the barn together. Neither one wanted to let go, wishing it could always be like this.

"If we did run away, where would you want to go?"

Tyler looked up at Ethan. His eyes were closed, and he had a look of bliss on his face with his tousled hair and peaceful smile. "I don't know."

"There has to be someplace."

"Just away from here. Far, far away from Cedar Creek."

"Okay, let's do it. Let's leave."

"Ethan..."

"I know I'm being silly, Tyler."

"It's not that. I would love nothing more."

Ethan smiled and kissed his lover.

"But Ethan, we can't. I got no job and my dad...he would find us, and he will murder us. I can't stand to see you hurt."

Ethan sighed and looked down at Tyler's soft golden hair and ran his hand through it. "Yeah, I know. I want to take you away from this place so badly. This town doesn't deserve you. I just want to be your knight in shining armor."

Tyler kissed his bare chest.

"But you already are."

Ethan stood up and pulled his shirt back on, as did Tyler. Tyler was sad to see his body disappear beneath the barrier of clothing. They walked into the house and towards Ethan's bedroom. From beneath the bed he pulled out the stuffed animal and hand it over to the boy. Tyler smiled, hugging the toy. The stuffed dog was soft and smelled like Ethan.

"He's cute. What's his name?"

"Whatever you want to name him. I got him for you."

"He looks like a Sam to me."

Ethan smiled and kissed his forehead.

"Then Sam it is. I got him so that way when I'm not around you can cuddle up to him and hug him tight. He will make sure you're never alone, okay?"

Tyler nodded and thanked him with a soft kiss. They lied in bed and fell asleep together. Tyler slept with his head on Ethan's chest and Ethan slept with his arms around the boy's slim body.

FOURTEEN

Michael walked in later that night. Cynthia was relaxing in the den with a book and greeted him with a kiss. He walked upstairs to his bedroom to change. Erin was pissing him off today and he needed to relax. She was going on about that David fellow all day. He was an asshole to them and had no respect for the law, but Erin whined how something was wrong.

Women.

As he walked past his son's bedroom he stopped and peaked inside. The door was slightly open, and, in the bed, he found the boys asleep. They were holding one another. Michael stepped back, closing the door all the way. What the Hell did he just see? His son shouldn't be cuddling with another man! He knew that gay boy was a bad influence on his family. He knew it! He walked downstairs into the den.

"Cynthia, we have a problem."

"What? Is everything okay?"

"Why is our son asleep with another man?"

Cynthia rolled her eyes. She knew this was going to

come out eventually and she wanted to protect her son for as long as she possibly could.

"You know how hard of a time Tyler has been having, with that abusive asshole he lives with." Even calling him a father filled her up with disgust.

"That's not what I mean, Cindy. Why are they asleep, holding one another?"

"Why do you say it like that?"

"Like what?"

"Like you just witnessed a murder."

"He's our son. He shouldn't be acting like that with another boy. It's not right."

"Says who?" she asked. Where was all this coming from? She felt the rage form in the pit of her stomach. She couldn't let it explode. She must not let it explode.

"It's just not right. A man should be with a woman, Cindy."

"What if Tyler makes our son happy? Wouldn't you want him to be happy?"

Michael looked away and leaned up against the table. What could he say to that? Ethan couldn't be happy with another boy. It ain't right. Why did his wife seem so okay with it? He shook his head and looked into Cynthia's eyes.

"I think it is time for Tyler to go home, Cynthia."

"No!" she yelled.

Michael nearly jumped at her booming voice. Where had that come from? All their years of marriage she had been a faithful, quiet woman. Now she was an animal.

"I cannot let you send that boy home. You'll be sending him to his death."

"Don't tell me what to do, Cynthia! I'm your husband. I'm the man in this house. I forbid Ethan from seeing Tyler."

"If you do that, I will leave you and take the kids with me, including Tyler."

"Are you threatening me?"

Cynthia took a deep breath and closed her eyes. "It's not a threat. It's an ultimatum."

Upstairs Tyler and Ethan woke up listening to the older couple's voices. Ethan held Tyler close as he heard the sheriff yell. Tyler was splitting apart Ethan's family. How could he stay here when he was ruining something great?

The fight didn't end until Mr and Mrs Gardner went to bed. Unknown to the boys, the sheriff slept downstairs on the couch that night. The house became silent and Ethan fell asleep again. Tyler looked over at the sleeping form of the man he loved. He looked so beautiful as he slept, and Tyler was a blemish on his wonderful life. No longer, could he stand to do that. He snaked out from Ethan's arms and packed up his bag, including the stuffed animal. Tyler didn't put his shoes on right away. He waited until he was out of the house.

He didn't cry as he walked the long four miles home. The night air was cold, and the wind froze his skin. He pulled up the hood of his sweatshirt and held onto his backpack with both hands. He was glad he didn't cry. He felt that was all he did in his life nowadays. Cry and feel bad. He hated how he always felt like a victim. He didn't want to be one anymore. He wanted to escape his life and not worry about drunk fathers, beatings, or bullying.

He reached his out as the sun began to rise. He didn't dare enter the house as his father would be getting ready for work at the time. Underneath his window was a rose trellis, which he used to climb up. His window was never locked. He pushed it up and crawled inside. After closing the window, he kicked off his shoes and stripped naked, slipping into bed. Sleep came fast to him that morning, but as he fell asleep, Ethan was waking up.

At first Ethan thought Tyler was possibly using the restroom. He woke up around 6am, alone in the bed. It was a small bed, but he had gotten used to the closeness of Tyler's warm body. But Tyler never returned to bed. He nervously played with the ring he always wore, before standing up. He noticed all his things were gone. He dressed and ran outside. He was nowhere to be found. How did he escape in the night? Why didn't he feel his best friend sneak out from his grasp? He should have woken up. God, damn it, he should have woken up.

He ran back into the house and woke his parents.

"Mom! Dad, Tyler is gone. He left in the middle of the night."

Cynthia jumped up. She knew where he went. He went back home, but why? The fight. He must have heard she and Michael fighting the prior night. Fuck! She hugged her son.

"It'll be okay. You can go get him today. You can bring him back, okay?"

Ethan nodded, feeling tears in his eyes. He was never one to cry. He hated crying. His father once told him as a child only wimps cry, and Ethan was no wimp. He quickly wiped his tears away before his father noticed.

"Let him be."

Cynthia and Ethan looked over at the patriarch of the family.

"How can you say that?" Ethan asked.

"This isn't his home. We are not his family. Frank is his father."

Cynthia couldn't believe she let him back into the bed in the middle of the night. She loved her husband, but this man was not her husband. He was an asshole.

"Michael, leave the room. Go back to your couch."

"This is my house. I'm staying in bed. I've got to sleep."

Cynthia stood up, taking her pillow and a throw blanket off an armchair in the corner of the room. Without a word, she shut the door and followed Ethan downstairs. They sat on the couch and as the sun finished rising, they discussed what they could do.

TYLER WOKE up in the early noon and stretched his limbs. He had gotten used to sleeping with Ethan in his bed. Now he felt lonely. He reached over and pulled Sam out of his backpack and held the plush dog close to his chest. He turned over to his side and looked out the window. Another sunny day outside. June had come to an end and July was popping into say hello.

He just wanted to stay in bed and do nothing all day. His father was at work and Ethan wasn't here. Tyler never had any other friends, and never really needed any others, but today he wished he had more friends. He wanted to talk about Ethan and his family with someone, but with who? He couldn't talk about them to Ethan. Tyler really appreciated them letting him stay there for a while, but he was a fool to think they'd let him stay forever. In the end, they weren't his family. He had no family. No family. No friends. He had Ethan, but what exactly was he to him? He still had no idea. Boyfriend? Best friend?

Maybe just a good fuck.

Ridiculous! I know I'm more than that to Ethan. If I was just a fuck for him, then he wouldn't still be around. He wished he knew what they were to one another. As is, he felt lost in the haze of love. Did Ethan love him too? Perhaps it was just lust.

The more he pondered, his head began to hurt. Soon it was pounding in his head. It felt as if his brain was smashing a hammer against his skull. Tyler stood up and pulled on pajama pants. They hung low on his slim waist. He walked to the kitchen and grabbed aspirin from a cupboard and took it with the water from the sink. Around his neck hung his amethyst crystal. He held it in hand and rubbed the crystal in his palms. Amethyst was supposed to help with depression. Nicole believed in all that bullshit about crystal healing, but sometimes he was desperate for help. She made him the necklace. Sometimes he believed it did help. He dropped the crystal, letting it fall past his chest.

A knock came at the door. Outside was Ethan. Tyler opened the door and Ethan pulled him into a tight hug, nearly crushing his ribs.

"Why the Hell did you leave?"

"You heard your father as well as I did. He didn't want me around. He doesn't want you being my friend. I can't be around your family and know I'm the reason they're falling apart."

"Shut up, Tyler! Fuck my father and fuck his beliefs. My mother loves you. Grace thinks your wonderful, and I, um. I lo, like you. A lot. You're my person, my rock."

Tyler smiled down at him but shook his head. "I'm going to stay here. I like you a lot too, but your father is right. You guys aren't my real family. I don't belong there."

"And you don't belong here," Ethan retorted.

"I don't belong anywhere."

"That's not true. You belong with me."

Tyler sighed and let Ethan hug him. Tyler felt a wave of content wash over his body, but he still couldn't go back with them.

"Please come back with me."

Tyler kissed him. "I can't."

FIFTEEN

Days went by with Tyler back at home. His father hadn't improved. His dad worked, drank, and abused him. The beatings were nearly every night. He was pissed about Tyler leaving. How could he leave him to fend for himself? On his second day back, his father sent him to the store to shop for food, giving him some of the cash from his savings. He needed to get that money back. It was his. How did he go about getting it? That is if he didn't spend all the money on booze.

He has been home for a week now and regretted coming home. Where could he possibly go? He couldn't live off the Gardners forever. Sheriff Gardner didn't even want Ethan associating with him.

Tyler lied down on his bed and held the stuffed dog close to his body. He breathed it in, but it was starting to lose the scent of Ethan, like an evaporating raindrop. He still wished he knew what exactly what they were to one another, but he made Tyler happy. When he was with Ethan, he could forget all about Cedar Creek. He wanted to see him.

. . .

ETHAN WAS UP EARLY that morning. He sat with Marshmallow and spoke to her. He wished she could answer back and give him the advice he needed. Ethan had never been so disappointed with his father like he was in that moment. His father was the damn sheriff. How could he send Tyler back to a place that was literally killing him?

"Marshmallow, what do I do?"

The horse whinnied, and Ethan smiled. He liked to pretend she understood him. As a child he wished he could talk to animals. It was a silly thing to wish for, he knew, but a part of him still wished he could.

"Ethan!"

He stood up from the stables and walked outside to find Tyler running towards the farmhouse. His long legs carried him, and his shirt was soaked with sweat. Ethan ran outside and pulled the boy into his arms. Tyler wrapped his legs around Ethan's waist and kissed him. Ethan adjusted his hands, so they were beneath Tyler's bottom.

"This is crazy, but I missed you. I haven't heard from you in days and my mind went to the worst places."

"I'm sorry. My father is out, so I got up and ran. My heart is racing. I think I need some water."

Ethan laughed and put the man down. Grabbing his hand, he pulled him into the kitchen and poured him a glass of water. Tyler downed it but needed more. His breathing was fast, a bit worrisome for Ethan. He pulled out the entire pitcher and left it on the table for him. Ethan watched him drink glass after glass of water and smiled. One would think Tyler had been living in the desert for the past year. When the pitcher was nearly gone, Tyler looked into Ethan's eyes and the two laughed. His laughter turned into a grimace.

"What's wrong?"

"It's nothing," Tyler replied. He didn't want Ethan to worry about his new bruises.

"Let me see."

Ethan got up and pulled up Tyler's shirt. His stomach was bruised everywhere. He was more bruise than skin.

"My God, Tyler."

Tyler pushed his hands away and let his shirt fall. He looked away from those chocolate eyes. He didn't want to see his pity. He wouldn't be able to hand any pity from him.

"You need to come here. Or call the police."

Tyler laughed. "You mean the police run by your father. The man who sent me back to Frank. They wouldn't do a thing to help. Trust me."

"We could run away together? I know I've said it before, but maybe we could really do so. No one would know us, and we could be together and out in the open."

"With what money?"

"I saved up some money from working on the farm and then there is the money you saved from working."

Tyler shook his head. "Frank took all the cash I saved.

"Tyler," he sighed. "I worry. I'm afraid that one day he'll go too far and you..." Ethan didn't want to finish the thought. He got onto his knees and rested his head upon Tyler's lap. He wasn't one to cry, but he needed to hold onto him. He couldn't let Tyler go. He knew things were going to get worse and he refused to lose his best friend and the man he liked. Maybe loved?

"It'll be okay." Tyler smoothed Ethan's hair down, running his long thing fingers through the thick mop of hair. He listened to the small moans, which escaped his mouth. "Ethan."

"Yeah?"

"What exactly are we?"

Ethan lifted his head up and looked up at Tyler. Tyler wasn't watching him; instead he was looking out the window in the kitchen.

"So, what are we?" Tyler repeated. This question had been bugging him for too long now. In secret they were together, but in public they were friends. If Tyler didn't get an answer soon, he was afraid he'd die from overthinking their relationship.

"What do you mean?"

"You're my best friend, but are we boyfriends? Friends with benefits? Are we monogamous?"

Ethan let out a deep breath and thought about the question. Tyler grew nervous, waiting for his answer. What could he be thinking about? The silence was barely a minute, but to Tyler and his overworking brain, it felt like months passed by before Ethan finally spoke.

"Do you want to be my boyfriend?"

"I mean, I guess. Do you?"

Ethan shook his head and laughed. "No, I'm asking you to be my boyfriend."

"Wait, really?"

Ethan smiled, "Yeah." He bit his lip as Tyler finally looked down into his eyes. He grabbed Tyler's hands in his and cleared his throat. "Let's try this again. Tyler Andrew Wuerth, would you do me the honor of being my official boyfriend?"

Tyler kissed him on the lips and whispered, "You're such a goofball sometimes."

"So, is that a yes?"

"Yes!"

Tyler hugged Ethan and breathed in his scent, thanking God for bringing Ethan into his life. He only wished they could be like this all the time. In the town, Ethan didn't pretend to be straight, but he wasn't exactly leading a pride parade either. In the past the sheriff would tell him about girls, and Tyler knew Sheriff Gardner would not be happy about the situation, but Tyler knew what it was like to be outed. He wanted Ethan to be comfortable. He loved him, and Ethan wanted to be with him. That was perfect.

Outside the kitchen entrance, the sheriff stood in his pajamas. Not a hint of emotion could be read on his face. He stood there, stunned. What did he just witness? His son couldn't be a queer. He knew the fairy would be a bad influence on his son. He knew it.

THE NEXT WEEK was nothing but bliss for the young lovers. They spent every waking moment together, especially in Neverland. They loved to swim and feel the sun tan their naked skin. They loved feeling one another's nude bodies in the small apartment as they dried off in one another's arms. They were happy. Truly and deeply happy.

Nothing could harm them. At least that is what they thought. On a chilly July night, everything would change for them. Their worlds would be shattered, and nothing would be able to save them from their incoming fates.

CHAPTER

SIXTEEN

Tyler's father was gone for the night. He went out with a one of the hicks on the town. She wasn't exactly pretty. Her name was Lynn. She was fifty years old but appeared to be eighty. She looked like a woman who spent a life smoking crack. Her thin frame was considered desirable by the drunks and hillbillies in Cedar Creek. Frank was the lucky man tonight to be taking her to bed. Tyler was home alone, drinking from a mug of tea he had made, while Frank fucked the woman, who was so out of it, she didn't even know who she was having sex with.

Tyler spent the day with Ethan. He woke up early to find Ethan waiting outside, leaned up against his pick-up truck. They went back to the farm, where Ethan showed him how to brush Marshmallow. Tyler smiled as he held the girl's brush in his hand and listened to her happy whinnies as he brushed her side. The horse reminded him of Ethan in a way.

Ethan watched Tyler brush his little girl. He could get used to a sight like that. Owning his own farm and having his own animals. Tyler would be by his side and together they'd be happy with all their animals. Ethan would make sure Tyler would never remember or feel the pain he faced each day. Tyler would be loved and feel nothing but love.

Ethan took Marshmallow outside and Tyler sat down on the fence as he watched Ethan ride her. Ethan held onto the strap and the horse galloped, her head high and her eyes closed. Her mane danced in the wind. Majestic, was the only word that came to Tyler's mind.

Ethan was the cowboy hero riding his steed and Tyler was the one he was on his way to rescue. He didn't want to be the damsel in distress, but Ethan really was his hero. He helped him escape the monster that controlled his life.

The day turned to night, and Ethan drove Tyler back home. Frank's car wasn't there.

"Thank you for today," Tyler said.

"It's not over yet. I want to come inside with you. While he isn't home."

Tyler smiled and nodded, leading his boyfriend inside and up into his bedroom. Together they lied down on his bed and closed their eyes. Tyler lied his head on Ethan's chest, while Ethan wrapped his big muscular arms around Tyler's slim frame. Tyler opened his eyes and looked up at Ethan's calm face. He kissed his neck, getting a moan from his cowboy. Ethan kissed him on the lips. Slow and easy at first. They held hands as they took their time. Neither one wanted to end the kiss, each boy afraid their time together had only been a dream.

Ethan deepened the kiss and Tyler kissed Ethan back, feeling his hands on his smooth slim body beneath his shirt. He unbuttoned Tyler's shirt, feeling each toned muscle. Tyler broke the kiss and watched Ethan whip off his tee shirt. His body was tanned and muscular. Covered in sweat and had a smell of hay.

"You're beautiful," Ethan whispered.

Tyler looked away and blushed. His blonde hair fell into his eyes. He wished Ethan would not say things like that. He knew that wasn't true. He was not beautiful. He was awkward. Weird, lanky. Definitely not beautiful.

"What's wrong?"

Tyler looked right into Ethan's soft brown eyes. Like chestnuts. They were so rich with a hint of red, the kind of eyes a boy could get lost in.

"I wish you wouldn't say things like that," Tyler admitted.

"Why? It's the truth."

"Stop it!" Ethan jumped at the thunderous reply. "I am not beautiful, Ethan." Tears flowed down his cheeks. Why did he always cry? He hated crying.

Ethan's heart sank in his chest. How could he think that way? Tyler was the most wonderful man he knew. He didn't know what to say, but his body worked faster than his mind. He pulled Tyler into a hug and ran his hands through his thick blonde hair. He felt the boy's hot tears on his bare chest.

"It's okay, I'm here. I'm here, Tyler."

The young men stayed like that for what felt like a lifetime. Ethan rubbed soothing circles on the other man's back. Ethan pulled away and looked up at Tyler. He reached up and wiped his tears away and pulled his face down towards him. He kissed each one of Tyler's closed eyelids, tasting the salty residue.

"I love you, Tyler."

Tyler opened his eyes. "What?"

"I love you," Ethan repeated. His voice was soft, just above a whisper.

"I love you too. I have for a long time."

The boys smiled and kissed one another. The kiss was wild, hungry. They've kissed before, but never like this. This was the kind of kiss that could make someone faint. They were starving for one another, and without the other's kiss they would die. Their tongues met and their fingers roamed. As they kissed, they felt their souls leave their bodies, reaching another echelon of spirituality, like astral projection.

Ethan rolled on top of Tyler. Tyler grasped for Ethan's jeans and awkwardly unbuttoned them, his fingers fumbling. His body shivered. Ethan smiled and slid his jeans down, kicking them to the ground. He kneeled on the bed in his underwear.

"Wow," Tyler gulped.

Ethan kissed his neck, leading a trail down his chest, taking each nipple into his mouth, making sure to suck on each one. He listened to Tyler's soft moans and continued down. Tyler closed his eyes and gripped his bed sheets. He bit his bottom lip to stop the scream from escaping his lips. He knew his father was out, but he still feared he would somehow hear them, and everything would be over.

He opened his eyes and saw Ethan unbuttoning his pants.

Tyler's cock throbbed as Ethan threw his pants onto the floor. Tyler lied there in his briefs. Tyler took a deep breath as Ethan kissed his quivering bulge. Ethan looked up and waited and his lover nodded. With that, he slipped off Tyler's briefs.

"I love you so much."

"I love you too," Tyler replied with a smile.

Ethan wrapped his lips around Tyler's erection, and Tyler moaned loudly. He no longer cared if anyone heard him. Fuck his Dad and this shitty town they lived in!

Ethan's head moved up and down, his warm tongue licking Tyler's length.

"Ethan," he moaned. "That feels so good!"

Ethan couldn't help but feel proud of himself, so he sucked faster. Tyler cried out, gripping his sheets so tight, his knuckles turned white. Tyler started to feel something, like he was going to burst soon. But he couldn't. Not yet. He wanted to make this last as long as he could.

"Wait, stop! You're gonna make me cum."

Ethan took his mouth away a kissed Tyler's lips gently.

"I want to make you feel good," Ethan whispered. His breath was hot on Tyler's ear. He wanted to respond, but all Tyler could do was nod. Nothing felt real to him.

A chill ran up Tyler's spine, as Ethan kissed down his back. He looked back and saw Ethan look up at him and smile. Ethan continued to kiss down Tyler's back. Ethan's heart welled up with all the love he felt for his best friend, his boyfriend. He wished this moment could last forever. Ethan wanted Tyler more than anything in the world.

TYLER BIT down on the pillow as Ethan's tongue entered him. No guy has ever made Tyler feel this way. Not even Beau.

"I WANT you to make love to me."

Ethan parted, and Tyler turned his head around to look at him. Tyler was shaking, covered in sweat. His eyes were big, magnified by his round glasses.

"You sure?"

Tyler nodded. "Yeah."

Ethan grabbed a condom from his wallet. He took in

Tyler's beautiful naked body. He would do anything for him. If Tyler asked him for the moon, Ethan would find a way to bring it to him.

Ethan pulled the condom on and entered Tyler. He heard Tyler grimace, and stopped.

"Are you okay?"

"It hurts a bit," Tyler admitted.

"I can stop."

Tyler shook his head. "No, please keep going."

Ethan nodded and took it slow.

Tyler was tight, but he felt like the perfect fit. Like a sword entering a sheath. He listened to his soft moans, loving that he was the cause of them. The feeling was electric. Their bodies connected in a way neither could have ever imagined. They were meant to be together. At first awkward, their bodies came together creating a perfect harmony. They were two instruments creating a symphony.

Ethan turned Tyler around. He wanted to look at him. He wanted to to kiss him. Tyler's hair was caked to his forehead with sweat. His cheeks were red, and his eyes were closed. His full lips were slightly parted.

"You're beautiful," Ethan whispered. "You're beautiful. You're beautiful. You're beautiful."

It became a mantra he needed to tell Tyler. He wanted him to feel loved. He wanted him to feel his love. Tyler felt every emotion pass between their bodies. Tyler smiled up at Ethan. The pain was gone. It had subsided to pleasure, and he never wanted Ethan to leave.

· · ·

The feeling was amazing for both of them.

Their bodies rocked with one another, their whispers of love filling the silence, until they both reached orgasm. They fell onto the bed beside one another, their chests heaving up and down. Neither of the young men spoke at first. All they could hear was the other's breathing.

"Wow!"

"Yeah," Tyler agreed.

"I love you."

"I love you too," Tyler spoke back before giggling. Ethan began to giggle too. Neither could believe that just happened. They relaxed as Tyler cuddled into his lover's body. Ethan kissed his forehead. Ethan dozed off as Tyler kissed his chest and listened to his heartbeat. Tyler closed his eyes and let himself drift off into sleep. At that moment, he felt safe. Tranquil. Sometimes tranquility ended, and Tyler knew that his nightmare would begin again, but not now. Not tonight. Tonight, it was all about he and Ethan. And their love.

Tyler and Ethan lied in bed together. Their naked bodies were tangled. There arms wrapped around one another and Tyler had his head resting on Ethan's chest, while Ethan ran his hands through Tyler's thick blonde hair. Their legs were a tangle of limbs. No one would be able to figure out where one began and the other ended. They were connected. Two souls that had finally found one another.

"How was that?" Ethan asked.

"Great! Was I okay?"

Ethan smiled and kissed his lips, "You were amazing. Absolutely amazing."

. . .

Tyler smiled, proud of himself. He kissed Ethan softly on the mouth, breathing in his lover's scent. A mix of sweat and hay. Not the most attractive smell, but to Tyler it was the aroma of Heaven. Ethan closed his eyes and kissed the top of Tyler's head. Tyler closed his eyes and listened to his rhythmic breathing, which turned into a light snore. His snores were different from his father's. Frank's snores sounded like a vicious bear. They were loud and angry, while Ethan's snores were soft and gentle, almost like a puppy. The room was blistering hot and their naked bodies were sticky with sweat. Tyler was never able to sleep in a hot room, but tonight he didn't want sleep. He wanted to remember every little detail about this night. Ethan's snores, the way the moon shined through the window, how Ethan's body fit perfect with his, the first time they made love.

Tyler was afraid to fall asleep, still believing this could be one long dream.

He couldn't help but think, every dream must come to an end.

SEVENTEEN

The boys woke up to a loud bang. The door slammed the wall, the knob breaking the wall. Frank grabbed Tyler by his hair and ripped him from the bed. He cried out as his shoulder exploded with pain when he collided with the wall.

"Leave him alone," Ethan shouted as he jumped out of bed. Tyler grabbed a pillow and covered himself. Ethan didn't care. He stood there naked as he stared into Tyler's father's cold eyes.

Frank's eyes were drunk and crazy. Veins popped out in his neck and his face was a disgusting shade of red.

"You," he pointed at Ethan. "Get out! A pair of fags in my home. Disgusting!"

Ethan balled his hands into fists and narrowed his eyes. No one was going to talk to him and Tyler like that.

"Are you going to hit me, fairy?"

Tyler looked up at Ethan with big wet eyes. He shook his head and pleaded.

"Ethan, go."

"Tyler?"

"Please, just go home."

Ethan looked at Tyler's face and bit his lip. He didn't know what to do, so he grabbed his clothes and ran out of the house. He didn't want to leave, but Tyler...

Ethan pulled on his clothes and jumped into his truck. He looked back at the farmhouse and drove off. What the Hell was he doing? Tyler needed him, and he ran away. He was no hero. He was a fucking coward.

Tyler sat in a ball on the floor, naked and vulnerable. His father looked down at him as if he was a fly that needed to be crushed beneath his boots. He spit at the boy. Tyler cried as the slobber landed on his face.

"Put some clothes on. You disgust me." Frank kicked his son in the stomach and listed to Tyler's painful scream, before leaving. Tyler cried on the floor. He didn't want to move. Everything hurt. His body, his head, his heart. He knew it was all too good to be true. Every dream had to end, and the monster had returned to bring him back into the nightmare.

ETHAN PARKED outside his house and slammed his steering wheel. He screamed and cursed. Why did he leave? This was what he was afraid of. The day Frank would go too far. What if Ethan never saw Tyler again? Worse: what if the next time he saw him was in the casket of his funeral.

Ethan walked into the house and up to his bedroom, ignoring his parent's calls for him. Coward! Tyler asked him to leave, and he did. But he shouldn't have. They spoke about running away, and Ethan wished it was possible.

His parents fought in the kitchen below his bedroom. He could catch a word here and there and knew the fight was about him. His mother was happy he found love, but his father not so much. Ethan never loved his mother so much as he did right there.

He could hear his father's shouts. He could no longer allow him to tarnish his reputation. The louder his father shouter, the more he heard of the fight.

"He's your son!"

The next thing to come out of his father's mouth was to break his heart.

"He's no son of mine. I will not have him live under my room."

Ethan's heart sank. He couldn't have really said that, could he? Maybe he imagined that. Every other word of the conversation no longer mattered.

Why was running away impossible? It didn't have to be. He had a little money saved up. They could find a place and they'd work. Escaping didn't have to be a fantasy. He had to go back for Tyler. He couldn't leave him there like that. An image shot through his head of him on the floor, naked and bruised. Fuck! I have to get him. We're leaving.

He grabbed a backpack and began to shove clothes inside. As the fight ended, he waited until his parents went to bed, and he snuck through the house and left his car keys on the kitchen table. He wrote a note, mostly for his mother. He no longer cared what his father thought, but as he wrote his note, his father appeared in the doorway, along with his mom.

"What's going on?" she asked.

Ethan took a deep breath, closed his eyes, and said good-bye.

TYLER'S TEARS HAD STOPPED, and he lied on his bed in the dark room. He didn't remember getting into the bed. The night had become a blur. He heard drinking in the kitchen, a reminder that he'd never escape this. He was stuck here. He was a tree, roots firmly planted into the ground of this house.

A knock came at his window. He didn't see anyone. A small pebble hit his window. He opened it and found Ethan outside holding a backpack.

"Ethan, you came back?"

"Of course, I did. Pack your bags. We are leaving."

Was this for real? Were they really going to leave Cedar Creek? Tyler pulled on clothes and packed a bag. He filled up a backpack and a suitcase with his belongings. He ran into the bathroom and collected his toothbrush and tooth-paste and his hair product. As he ran around, a strange excitement filled his body. He and Ethan were going to start a life together. A real life away from this place. Tyler grabbed his bags and ran downstairs.

Frank stood at the bottom of the stairs, whiskey bottle in hand.

"Where the fuck are you going?" His breathe wreaked of whiskey and cigarettes.

Tyler swallowed the lump in his throat. "I'm leaving." He mustered up all the strength he could manage. His father laughed. Tyler walked down the stairs. Frank watched his son and slammed the alcohol bottle across his head. Tyler fell to the ground. Liquor stained his clothes and blood ran down his forehead.

"I hate you," Tyler spit with venom in his voice. The words were like vomit. They fell right out of his mouth, and the moment they left his mouth, he regretted it.

Frank spit on him and grabbed his arm, punching him in the face. Tyler fell to the ground, his hands going into the broken glass, shredding apart his skin. Frank grabbed his think mop of blonde hair and dragged him across the ground. Tyler screamed and begged for his father to stop.

Frank leg go and kicked him in the side. Tyler's glasses flew off his face, but Tyler refused to cry. Not for this asshole. Never again. His father pummeled him, but not one tear escaped. No longer would he give into this man. No longer would he allow him to see his weakness. It was over. Tyler couldn't take it anymore and he pushed his father to the ground. Tyler gasped at what he did. He grabbed his glasses and stoop up, ignoring the pain.

"I hate you," and this time he meant to say it. "I am leaving, Frank, and I'm never coming back. Your faggot son is leaving. Good-bye." Tyler walked towards the front door and left the place he once called home. His father stood up and ran for the door.

"Get back here, faggot! If you don't come back here, I will beat your fairy ass!" Tyler ran right into Ethan's arms. Tyler smiled as exhilaration charged through his bones like a river rushing to the sea. He slammed his mouth onto Ethan's and kissed him home.

"Baby, are you okay?" Ethan grabbed Tyler's face and stared at his black eye and his bloody face. His lip was split open but, Tyler smiled.

"I've never felt better. I love you so much, Ethan!"

Ethan's face lit up. He lightly brushed his bruised face and kissed him.

"I love you too."

They grabbed hands, fingers lacing together, and the two young lovers ran off into the night. No longer would they live in this bad dream of a life.

CHAPTER

EIGHTEEN

Ethan held Tyler's bloody and bruised face in his hand in the bathroom of a gas station. Why did he leave him? Tyler's face was disturbing to look at.

"I am so sorry. I should never have left you."

"It's okay. You came back," Tyler said with a bloody smile.

Ethan cleaned up his face. There was nothing to be done for the black eye, but the blood was gone. He placed the glasses back on Tyler's face and kissed him.

"I love you."

Tyler smiled. "I love you too."

His body ached but he didn't care, now that it was only he and Ethan. He hugged him tight and closed his eyes. He couldn't believe they were actually running away. It was a dream. He was finally leaving the town and the monster that haunted his nightmares. And he was doing it with Ethan.

They left the station and the boys walked along the lonely dark road towards the unknown. Maybe they should have waited for morning. The night air was cool, and Ethan wore a flannel, while Tyler wore a hoodie. It was a crazy day for both Tyler and Ethan. What started off as the perfect day ended in disaster. They were the Titanic and Frank was the iceberg. Ethan had wished he took the truck, but his father paid for it, and he couldn't take it in fear of him coming after them.

Ethan let out a sigh. "My father overheard us."

Tyler's heart grew heavy sinking into his stomach. It felt like it was about to be dissolved in the acids of his stomach.

"He did?"

"Yeah. They caught me writing a note in the kitchen as I was leaving. My mom was trying to stop me. Dad was pissed off and Mom tried to calm him down, but...my dad said he no longer had a son. He essentially kicked me out. Last I saw, Mom was fighting with him. I feel bad for leaving her and Grace."

Tyler let go of Ethan's hand and turned away. Was this really a good idea? Not only was his life ruined, but now he was ruining the life of the one person who had been there for him all along. "I am so sorry. This is my fault."

"Shut up! I am kind of happy. Everything is out in the open, and Tyler, I love you. I've been dreading this moment of coming out for so long, and now it's out and it's over."

"I love you too."

Ethan hugged him close to his body and they continued to walk hand in hand. He worried about Tyler. Ethan's father was an asshole, but Tyler's father was a monster. They'd never be apart. That, Ethan would be sure of.

There was nothing they could do now, other than walk. So, they kept on walking. The road was long and the houses far and few. Their only guiding light was from the stars above. The very thing Tyler prayed on. While God ignored his pleas, the stars watched over him each night and kept him from being alone.

Tyler grew tired as the night wore thin. He couldn't see the time on his watch, but it must have been incredibly late, or incredibly early. Ethan looked back and found Tyler a couple feet behind him. He stopped and waited for Tyler to catch up.

"You okay?"

"Never better."

"Let's stop and rest for a while," Ethan said. From the light of the moon, he could make out the exhaustion on his boyfriend's face. His eyes were only half open and every other sound that came out of his mouth was a yawn.

"You sure?"

Ethan smiled at him, pulling him close. He was sure. They set their bags down on the ground and lied on the side of the road. The grass was soft beneath their backs as they used their bags as pillows and cuddled up. It didn't take long for Tyler to fall asleep, his head on Ethan's chest. He hoped the boy dreamt well, but Ethan didn't think that'd happen. Tonight, was a struggle for them both, but especially Tyler. He rubbed the back of his head and closed his eyes.

Night turned to day as the sun rose in the sky. Neither of the boys woke up from the sun. It wasn't until later when Tyler stirred. He rubbed the sleep out of his eyes and fixed his glasses. Why did he sleep with them on? He looked around his surroundings. He wasn't in his bed? Where exactly was he?

Everything flooded back to him. All the memories of the night before. He had thought it was only a dream, but sadly it wasn't. He and Ethan were homeless and on the run like a pair of petty criminals. Their crime? Loving one another.

Ethan soon awoke, and they were back on the road.

KAITLYN PACKED up her bag and checked out of the motel. It was only around 9AM but it was a long drive ahead. Her car was saddled up and all she had to do was drive. She honestly loved driving, especially in the summer with the windows down and the breeze in her long dark hair, but even she was starting to grow tired of it. She was staying in the third motel this week. She was in some town called Melancholy. An appropriate name, she had to say. The town was barely a town. She could walk from one end to the other in a matter of an hour and no one seemed to leave their houses. A gray overcast stood over the town the entire day she stayed.

She turned on the car and pulled away from the seedy motel, happy to see it disappear in the rearview mirror. She grabbed a CD from the glove department and turned up the volume as Every Breathe You Take by The Police blasted out of the speakers. Her car vibrated as she raced down the road. She has had enough of the country music on the radio. She was definitely not a country girl. The City was in her blood.

The road was empty for long stretches of time. As Kaitlyn drove, she sung to the music and pulled on her sunglasses. She hoped to find herself on this journey, but she wished she brought a friend along. Sometimes the journey became lonely. No one to talk to but herself. She also could do with a shower. The motel's bathroom was too unsanitary. There was no way she could bathe in it. The water came out an amber color when she turned the shower on. Even with the breeze, her clothes stuck to her sweaty body and she could only put on so much perfume.

She passed a sign, welcoming her to the town of Cedar Creek. More farmland, but at least the sun was out, and the sky was blue. At first, she loved the rural setting, but she needed life again. She was starting to miss the busy hustle of New York City.

On the side of the road she watched as two young men put their thumb out. She raced past them and watched them in the side mirror. Why the hell not, she thought. She could use the company. She pressed down on the break and reversed up to the two young men. She opened her window.

"Where are you headed?"

THE SUN WAS hot as it burnt their flesh red. Ethan's skin baked into a golden brown with his perfectly tan skin. His shirt was off and hanging from his back pocket. Sweat dripped down his face and bare chest. His muscles glistened in the sun, like the cover model of a trashy sex novel.

Tyler rolled his sleeves up to his elbows. His bruises were much lighter. It has only been hours since they left home, and they were still walking into the unknown. Cedar Creek was all long stretches of road and farms. To their left was cornfields and to their right was more.

Tyler bent over to catch his breathe.

"Ethan, can we take a break?"

Ethan turned around and pulled out a water bottle from his bag. He handed it to Tyler.

"Yeah, of course. Drink some of this. Are you okay?"

Tyler nodded, "Yeah, just a little overheated. Thank you." He took a long sip of water and sat down on his suitcase. "Sorry, I just need a break."

"Don't apologize. It's okay." Ethan sat down on his

duffel bag and grabbed Tyler's hand. They cooked beneath the hot august sun and realized they were utterly alone out here. A car hasn't passed by in nearly an hour. The town was small, but it felt large when they walked. Southern heat wasn't like any other heat. It didn't just burn you, but it slow roasted you until you were well done. Especially for people with fair skin like Tyler. Ethan was one of the lucky people who tanned.

A red convertible drove past them. Ethan put out his thumb, but the car raced. Damn it, Ethan thought. The car stopped and backed up. The young men jumped up and grabbed their bags. The window rolled down and an attractive young woman with long dark hair sat behind the wheel. She pushed her sunglasses to the top of her head.

"Where are you headed?"

"Anywhere but here," Ethan answered.

"Get in then. It's hot as balls out here!"

Ethan laughed, "Yes, thank you!" Ethan threw their bags in the woman's trunk and they both got into the car. Ethan took the front seat and Tyler took the back. She drove off and Tyler felt the breeze from the opened windows. He closed his eyes and smiled. Ethan looked back and grabbed his hand and smiled. He squeezed Tyler's hand, letting him know they were okay. Tyler squeezed back.

"Thank you again, um..."

"Kaitlyn. Since I will be your chauffeur for the day, what are your names?"

Ethan liked her. "Nice to meet you, ma'am. I'm Ethan and this is my, um, this is Tyler."

Kaitlyn smiled in the rearview mirror. Tyler ripped his hand away from Ethan's. He didn't want to be thrown back into the heat.

"You two make a cute couple."

"You could tell," Ethan asked. His voice shook with anxiety.

"It's not a bad thing. The way you guys look at each other, I can just tell. You look at one another as if no one else in the world exists. Plus, you were holding hands. Do you love each other?"

The boys smiled and nodded. Ethan took Tyler's hand and kissed each one of his fingers.

"Very much."

They're adorable, Kaitlyn thought. She missed having that with someone, but she was happy to still see love was alive out there. That was when she noticed the quiet boy's face. The blonde had been beaten up. She lost her smile.

"Did Cedar Creek do that to your face, Tyler?"

Tyler looked down at the ground, as if he was ashamed. This woman was a stranger. How could he tell her about his sob story? "I guess you could say that," he answered with a deep sigh.

"When people fuck with you, you have to fuck with them right back. Trust me. I may be young, but I know a lot of shit."

Ethan smiled. Yeah, he really liked her. She felt modern, compared to everyone from their hick town at least. She drove through the country and let the boys relax. Judging by their exhausted faces and the bruises on the blonde, it's been a long day for them. The boy, Tyler, seemed so frightened. He reminded her of an abused puppy she found when she was a little girl. Someone beat and started the tiny dog and left him to die out in the sun. Kaitlyn and her sister rescued the dog and tried to save him, but it died the next day. It had broken her heart. Within a few hours she had fallen in love with the pup and promised to take care of him. Animals had an innocence about them that could make one fall in love much faster than they could with a human. They needed to be loved and protected, and that was the feeling she got from Tyler.

He needed to be protected.

She's known these young men for only a few minutes and she was already going into warrior mode to protect them. Her friends always said she got attached too quickly, and maybe they were right.

She looked into the rearview mirror and found the boy asleep in the backseat. His glasses were lopsided. She lowered the music and looked over at Ethan. He looked outside at the passing scenery.

For the first time that day, Ethan felt safe. They were on their way out of this damn town and towards their future. He didn't want to tell Tyler, but he was starting to regret the decision that morning. He needed to remain sure for Tyler. He couldn't let him worry about anything. Ethan would do the worrying. He only wanted to protect him. He watched him sleep in the rearview mirror, happy he could finally relax.

As the sun set, Kaitlyn found herself yawning. Why was she so tired today? She thought the company would help her wake up, but she found herself parking outside a motel in Cedar Creek. It was secluded and towards the other side of the town. After driving past all the farmhouses and corn-fields, she rolled up to the motel.

"Come on guys. I think you two deserve a good night's rest."

Ethan shook Tyler awake, who had been sleeping all day. Poor kid, she thought. He looked like he needed that. Ethan would stare at him with sadness and love in his eyes, the way a mother would look at a wounded child. She wanted to know what had taken place today, but she didn't want to overstep the boundaries.

"Where are we?" Tyler asked, his voice soft and groggy.

"We're at the motel. We are going to get some sleep, okay?" Ethan replied, holding onto his knee. Tyler nodded and rubbed his eyes.

They took their bags inside and Kaitlyn paid for two rooms. She refused to accept Ethan's money. They settled into their two rooms. Ethan and Tyler lied in bed and it didn't take long for Tyler to fall asleep. Ethan covered him with the blanket and kissed his forehead. He left the room and stood outside and let out his first sigh of relief. Kaitlyn stepped outside and joined him. She lit up a cigarette.

"So, what happened to you guys?"

Ethan smiled and shrugged his shoulders. "Life."

"A man of many words," she laughed.

He couldn't help a chuckle from escaping. "Sorry. It's been rough for Tyler and me. This town sucks and our fathers aren't any better. Tyler's father is a nightmare. I had to get him out of there."

"His father did that to him?"

Ethan nodded. She offered her cigarette and he took a long drag. He hadn't had one of these in a long time, but he needed one right now. She took a couple out of the box and gave them to him.

"Thanks." He lit up his own cigarette and sucked into the smoke, letting it fill his lungs. The feeling was nearly orgasmic as he let out the smoke. "I haven't had one of these in a long time. I forgot how good they were."

"They're bad for you."

He shrugged and sucked on it again, listening to the crisp crackle of the paper.

"Tell me what happened."

Ethan sighed. She wasn't one to let go, so he told her the story. He told her their love story and about their nightmare. As he spoke about Tyler's father, she felt disgusted. She had to light up another cigarette to get through the story. How could someone abuse their own son like that? It made no sense to her. She was lucky to live in such a liberal place.

As he finished the story, they stood there in silence. Neither knew what to say. The remnants of the memories he relived remained in the air like a foul smell that could not be erased.

"I think you guys deserve a little fun. Are there any gay bars or clubs in this town? Someplace you can relax, dance, and be open."

Ethan smiled, "That's nice of you to say, but I don't know. We never really had a chance to go out before. We went to the movies once? We usually stick to ourselves."

"Not tonight. I'm taking you boys out, okay?"

Kaitlyn gave him hope for the future. Being around her was what he needed. She was reminding him that it was a good idea they ran away. There will be people out there like her, once they completely escape. Maybe she was right. They did deserve one night out before they're on their way. Ethan pondered. "Well, there is one small gay bar not too far from this motel. I've heard about it, but never been. I never had the guts to go."

"Let's go tonight!"

"Where are we going?" Tyler responded, looking up at Kaitlyn. He pushed his round glasses up his thin nose. He stood in the entrance of his room, with the blanket wrapped around his shoulders.

She was going to show them a good time. She always had a good reading from people, and these boys needed some fun to get their minds off life. Especially Tyler. So, she told Tyler the plan.

Ethan liked the idea, while Tyler thought longer and harder. He wanted to get out of this town and never look back, but the idea did sound fun. So much has happened in just one night. He is running away with the love of his life and he stood up for his father. He was beginning a new life, so it was time to be a new person.

He bit his lip and nodded.

"Okay."

Ethan pulled him into a hug. Tyler couldn't say no to that. He loved making him happy. They went into their motel rooms and got ready. When they left it was around 10pm and they arrived at the gay bar by 10:25pm. Kaitlyn looked at the bar, and Ethan wasn't kidding when he said it was small. It was barely a shed. New York City had plenty of clubs and bars, and this place was the side of the bathroom in them.

As they walked through the barrier, they found a world of color. Tyler knew what Judy must've felt like leaving her house in Oz. His black-and-white world had become one of color. The bar was barely full of people. Behind the bar was an older man with a beard. He wore no shirt, showing off the slight muscles he had. Tyler nor Ethan recognized him. He must have been an out of towner.

"Tyler?" An older man with gray stubble and a pair of square glasses sat at the bar. It took a moment to recognize him, as it had been so long.

"Mr Wright?"

Tyler walked up to his old high school English teacher and looked at him. He looked exactly the same. His tee shirt clung to his muscular body and his jeans were tight, showing off the large bulge beneath.

"You can call me Nick now. I haven't been your teacher in at least two years."

Nick pulled Tyler into a hug and pulled out a seat next to him. Ethan and Kaitlyn sat down as well.

"Good to see you, Ethan."

Ethan responded with a nod in his direction. He never had him as a teacher. It was Tyler's junior year when Nicholas Wright was fired. It had come to light that he was a gay man, and the parents didn't want him teaching their children. They were afraid he'd either make their children gay or molest them.

"How have you been?" Tyler asked.

"Great. I'm working at a new school. I'm teaching English the next town over. I'm living with my partner now. Hey, Evan! This is Evan Dior."

Evan was a skinny man with dirty blonde hair and dark blue eyes. When he smiled, it took over his face. His eyes lit up and his teeth were white.

"This was my student Tyler, and his boyfriend?"

Tyler and Ethan nodded and smiled at one another. It felt nice to be out in the open and not have to hide their feelings. They can look at one another, touch one another, kiss one another. Ethan took Tyler's hand in his own and kissed it. As Tyler caught up with his old teacher, Ethan looked out at the bar. Rainbow flags were hung up on the walls and over the stereo system they were playing popular music that anyone could dance too. Madonna was currently begging for her papa not to preach.

A disco ball hung from the middle of the ceiling in the darkly lit room, along with a spinning ball of lights that flashed an array of colors along the bar's walls. Ethan always wondered about bar, but it was considered a joke to the town. The place was the only gay bar around for miles.

The towns surrounding Cedar Creek didn't have any. Built in 1970, the bar had become a sanctuary for abused or closeted gay men. He heard it was mainly a place for closeted married men to have quickies before going to bed with their clueless wives in the beds they shared. People in town laughed at the bar, vandalized the bar. But he was here now.

The bartender offered them drinks, without asking for ID. He winked at Ethan and poured three shots for them. Ethan and Kaitlyn downed theirs, but Tyler stopped and stared at his drink in the tiny glass.

"Don't be afraid, kiddo. It's just Whiskey."

Tyler didn't like the way alcohol affected his father. What if it did the same to him? He's read alcoholism could be hereditary, so what if he drank and turned into the very monster he was escaping. Ethan looked at him and smiled.

"It's okay if you don't want to."

Always so caring. Tyler wanted him to relax. He didn't always have to focus on Tyler, plus he deserved at least one crazy night in his life.

He downed the liquor. It burned his throat and he began to cough. Nick and Evan laughed along with the bartender and Kaitlyn. Ethan rubbed his back. The bartender poured another round of Whiskey and the trio drank them. This time Tyler prepared himself and didn't cough. The song changed and on came Tainted Love by Soft Cell. Tyler loved this song. He danced a little in his seat.

"You should go dance," Kaitlyn said.

On the floor a few couples danced closely, moving wild. Their limbs were noodles doing whatever they wanted. Tyler shook his head. He couldn't.

Ethan grabbed his hands, but Tyler stood his ground. Ethan pouted and began to dance on in front of him, stepping backwards. He bit his lip, swinging his pelvis as a few boys from the bar looked over. Tyler took another shot and stood up. His knees felt a bit weak and his brain was a tad woozy. This is how I feel when I have a cold, he thought.

He stood in front of Ethan and moved with the music. He tried to mimic Ethan's dancing. Ethan was in time to the music. His entire body screamed of rhythmic sex appeal. He licked his lips and couldn't believe that this man wanted him. He did deserve him. Why did he always feel like he didn't? He's not totally out of Cedar Creek yet, but the closer he gets, the more confident he becomes. He smiled and closed his eyes and stopped caring. He danced, letting loose. He didn't care about being one with the music. He did whatever felt right. He may look like a freakshow on the dancefloor, but it was his choice. He was doing what he wanted, and he was happy.

Happy. A word that didn't describe him often. Happiness, for Tyler Wuerth, was akin to a myth one tells around a campfire. Happiness was the transcendent plane he's never been able to reach. But here he was, and he was happy.

Truly, deeply, happy.

CHAPTER

NINETEEN

It was past 1am when Ethan and Tyler fell through the door of their motel room. Tyler felt light, as if he could float away. His hair was a mess and the top few buttons of his shirt were opened. Ethan helped him inside.

"Tonight, was fun," Tyler said.

"Yes, it was."

"You are so sexy. Oh my stars, how did I get so lucky," Tyler drawled.

Ethan laughed at his drunk boyfriend. He's never seen him this way and it was quite entertaining, he must say. He placed him down on the bed and kissed him. He helped undress him and took his glasses off. Tyler fell asleep soon after. Ethan took his clothes off and got beneath the covers and wrapped his arm around Tyler's waist.

KAITLYN STEPPED out of the shower. She had fun tonight. It was definitely not like any club she's been too, but there was something quaint about the bar. She didn't even know if it had a name. It had a rainbow flag in the window, and that was it. No sign or landmark stating what it is.

Watching Tyler loosen up, was like witnessing a whole new incarnation of a person, the way a caterpillar became a butterfly. The quiet scared boy she met earlier that day had spread his wings and flew right before her eyes.

Kaitlyn looked down at the sink and screamed as a spider crawled from the drain. She turned on the water and filled the wink with water. It picked the small tan spider up and Kaitlyn watched as all eight legs splashed the water, slapping, trying to stay afloat. She thought of the nursery rhyme.

The itsy-bitsy spider

Climbed up the water spout

As the waves of water crashed around it, the itsy-bitsy spider looked to be in such pain. She shut the water off in the sink. As the little whirlpool spun its deadly cycle, it took the spider around on the most terrifying amusement park ride.

Down came the rain

And washed the spider out

The water drained, and the little arachnid stuck to the sink like a beached whale. It was still moving, those disgusting little legs, but just barely. It brought up one thin, string-like leg, as if it was praying to God to save its life.

Out came the sun

And dried up all the rain

Kaitlyn found herself feeling guilty for the damn spider. She turned on the sink and washed it down the spout.

And the itsy-bitsy spider

Climbed up the spout again.

"Sorry, little guy, please don't climb up the spout again."

She turned off the water and pulled on a tank top and fleece shorts. She wasn't very tired, so she grabbed a book from her bag and lied down in the hard bed, which felt like rocks against her back.

Tyler woke up in the motel room and turned over to find the other side empty and cold. A street lamp from outside illuminated the room, casting a white glow onto Tyler's skin. He wrapped the quilt around his naked body and found Ethan outside in his briefs with a cigarette cuddled between his lips. Tyler saddled up beside his lover.

"You okay?"

Ethan threw the cigarette to the ground and gave Tyler a small forced smile, "Yeah."

"You only smoke when something is wrong. So, tell me what is upsetting you. Don't make me force it out of you."

Ethan smiled, "And how would you force it out of me?" Ethan winked at the taller young man.

Tyler rolled his eyes. "I'm being serious. What's wrong?"

"I am okay, just nervous. We are starting an entirely new life. I am excited, but terrified, Tyler. We have spoken about doing this for so long, but..." Ethan trailed off, all words disappearing from his head. Only a gray fog sat in his mind.

"It's okay. I feel the same way," Tyler admitted. "All my life, this town has tortured me, but I still feel like I am leaving something behind."

Ethan pulled Tyler close to him and kissed the top of his head.

"We'll be okay," Ethan promised. Tyler really hoped they would.

Ethan put out the cigarette and walked back into the motel room. He closed the door and watched Tyler drop the blanket. His naked body pale from the light outside. Beneath the white glow, he was an angel.

"You're so beautiful."

This time, Tyler didn't fight him. He pulled Ethan closed to him and kissed him. Ethan's underwear was gone, and it wasn't long before they were making love on the bed. The walls were thin and the bed uncomfortable, but neither cared. They wanted to show their love for one another and as Ethan thrusted into Tyler, Tyler let himself lose control. He held onto Ethan's shoulders, as his legs were slung over his shoulders. Together they moaned as Ethan moved inside him and Tyler moved towards him. He wanted to feel Ethan inside him. He loved the way he made him feel.

Ethan's mouth was on the boy's neck. Kissing, sucking, biting. He needed him like he needed air. Tyler moaned as he pushed his head back.

"I love you so much."

"I love you too," Tyler moaned.

Neither knew how much longer they could last in their time of ecstasy. Tyler grabbed onto Ethan's hand as they both came.

THEY COULD BARELY FEEL their bodies. Tyler sat up on his knees and stared into Ethan's eyes. They shared a kiss falling onto the bed. They stayed close, their hands roaming. They needed to feel one another's body. Caress it. Love it. They fell asleep in each other's arms, and when morning came, they made love once again in the shower.

CHAPTER
TWENTY

The sky was cloudy, when Kaitlyn woke up. She sat up stretched her limbs, listening to her aching bones crack. Only twenty-eight and she was already starting to feel her body change. Dancing at the bar with her new friends left her body sore that morning. She wanted to take more photographs before leaving, but the dark gray clouds threatened her with the oncoming storm.

In the room next door, Tyler and Ethan lied in bed. They were silent as they stared into one another's eyes. Their fingers caressed one another's bodies, feeling every nook, exploring one another. Their hair was wet from their shower.

"I wish we could stay like this all day," Tyler admitted.

"We will have days like this. Entire days just dedicated to studying each other's bodies," Ethan answered. "And we have right now."

Ethan grabbed his hand and laced his fingers through his. He has been studying his body so intensely, he knew it better than his own body. He knew every freckle, every blemish. He knew what spots made him feel good, and which made him laugh. Tyler was a book he couldn't stop reading. His body drove him crazy, and his mind was one worth exploring. He looked at their hands. Tyler's fingers were longer than his, but slimmer. Ethan's were shorter, but fatter. He traced a finger down the spine of his back, feeling each crevice, ending at the top of his bottom. He grabbed both cheeks in his hands, getting a moan from Tyler. They made love twice that day already. After the bar and in the shower that morning, and Ethan couldn't be any happier.

Soon they would have to leave. When the boys finally dressed, they met with Kaitlyn next door. The overcast day grew darker. Tyler wondered if they should stay one more day in the motel, but Ethan wanted to get back on the road.

They checked out of the tiny motel, and as they began to drive away, the rain fell. Ethan sat in the backseat with Tyler. Tyler held his lover's hand as they drove. The mid-July air was cool that day. Ethan wore a thick blue and black plaid flannel, while Tyler wore a dark red sweater over his light blue button-up shirt. Kaitlyn was surprised that she had to pull a cardigan out of her suitcase. Is the world trying to tell me to stay put? She quickly laughed off the thought. Impossible. It's just a little drizzle. No need to worry about it.

The light drizzle grew heavy through the day. Lightning flashed, and thunder roared. Tyler held onto Ethan's hand. Damn thunderstorms. He knew it was silly to be afraid of them, but he felt there was something unnatural about them, as if Lucifer was trying to strike him down.

The rain pelted the car like tiny icicles. With her lights on and the windshield wipers going full blast, Kaitlyn still couldn't see the road. The sky had grown dark.

No stars.

No moon.

Only darkness.

Kaitlyn never minded the rain, but as the thunder's roar exploded, she felt her heart hit her chest. What was wrong with her? It was just the rain. She usually liked the rain, but something about this storm felt like a warning. Stay away, it was telling her. But from what, she didn't know.

Streetlights disappeared, and the town was gone. Even the farmhouses were no more. All that surrounded them were fields of corn and wheat and trees. If something happens to us, no one would be around to help, Kaitlyn thought. She turned on the heat as a chill caressed her skin. She looked down to play with the dials.

"Watch out!" Tyler screamed.

Kaitlyn looked up and saw two headlights heading right towards her. She turned the steering wheel and the car swerved to the right, missing the other vehicle. The road was slick, and Kaitlyn couldn't control the wheel. She panicked as the car drove off the road. She did her best not to scream, but she lost. Her head crashed into the steering wheel as her car collided with a tree.

Kaitlyn woke up to Ethan shaking her shoulder. Fuck, my head is pounding.

"Are you okay?" he asked.

She nodded, pain shooting through her face. She brought her hand to her forehead, finding blood. What happened? She was driving and then...I crashed, right.

She turned around and found Tyler holding onto Ethan's hand.

"You guys okay?"

Tyler nodded.

"Yeah, we are fine," Ethan answered with a smile. "You don't look so good. You're bleeding."

"Yes, I figured that out for myself."

Ethan dug through his backpack and pulled out a bandana. She thanked him as she held it to her head. She had to remember to buy him a new bandana when they got out of this mess. When her head stopped feeling like a pair of rolling dice, she turned the key, but nothing happened.

No, this couldn't be happening. She turned the key again and the engine rolled but never came to life. Damn!

"Wait here. I will go check."

Tyler looked out the window and saw the sign. He almost had to laugh at their luck. He always felt the town was cursed, and now he knew he was right. Outside the window a street sign stood.

You're now leaving Cedar Creek.

This town was never going to let them leave, Tyler feared. They were going to be stuck here forever. Tyler was going to die in Cedar Creek.

Ethan jumped out of the car with a flashlight, from the glove compartment and ran to the front of the car in the pouring rain. The front of the car wrapped around the tree. Lightning flashed as he bent down to look at the wheels. They were sunk so far deep into the mud, that even if the car was okay, he didn't think they could leave with that.

Crunch.

Ethan spun around and looked into the cornfield. He could have sworn he heard something snap. It sounded like a twig. Maybe someone was out there. They might be able to get help.

"Hello," he called out. He waved his flashlight but saw no one. I guess not. He walked back into the car and sat in the backseat again.

"We are stranded."

"Is the car that bad?" she asked. She loved the car so much. Maybe it could be rescued.

"The car is a goner, I'm sorry."

Kaitlyn sighed. Good night. Sweet prince. You will always be remembered. This was the first car she ever bought and was still the only car she ever bought. She felt like she was losing a child, as stupid as that sounded to her.

"It looks like we are stuck here for the night. You guys want a threesome?" she joked. There was nothing else she could do, she might as well lighten the situation.

The boys smiled. Kaitlyn was happy to see the younger boy smile. Tyler's face completely changed when he smiled. His face looked childlike and innocent.

Hopefully another car would pass by soon, Tyler prayed. He didn't want to be stuck here any longer. As he looked out the window again, lightning flashed, and he saw someone! There was someone out there.

"Guys, I saw someone!"

"What? Where?" Kaitlyn asked.

They all looked out the windows and towards the cornfields, but no one could see anything.

"Maybe it was just an animal," Kaitlyn responded.

"No, I saw a person. When the lightning flashed, I am sure I saw a person. He was right there in the cornfield."

"I read somewhere that sometimes the dark can play tricks on your eyes. So, you might think you saw..."

"No!" Tyler hissed. "I know I saw someone. It was a man. It was only for a split second, so I didn't get a good luck, but there was something on his face. Maybe a mask? I don't know."

Kaitlyn stared at him, wide-eyed. She hadn't seen him

be so aggressive. It had surprised her. This boy was stronger than he looked. She was sure of it.

As Tyler looked for the man he saw, the Miller stood in the rain watching the broken-down car. He held his sickle in hand and studied the people inside, his eyes focused on the blonde boy with the big glasses.

TWENTY-ONE

8:33pm, the clock read in the car. Kaitlyn sighed. Not one car had passed on by, since the accident. They were practically alone. There might not even be a town full of people. For a small town, it felt giant.

Lightning flashed, and Kaitlyn could make out a building. She pointed at the building, "Wait, what's that?"

They all strained their eyes to see what she saw.

"I don't see anything," Ethan said.

"Just wait."

Lightning struck again and as the thunder roared Tyler noticed the hint of light in the distance.

"I see it! And there is a light on as well."

"We should head over there," Ethan stated.

Kaitlyn laughed. "In this rain?"

"They could have a phone," Tyler added.

Kaitlyn pondered this for a moment and agreed. They grabbed a flashlight from her car and the three of them stepped out into the pouring rain. Kaitlyn locked the car and they walked into the cornfield and towards the building in the distance.

The rain smacked them as they trampled through the mud and dirt. The rain was like ice on their skin. It soaked through their clothing and matted their hair to their faces. Each drop of hard rain was a slap to the face. They pushed the towering husks of corn away from their bodies, hoping they were heading in the right direction. The farther they walked, the slower they moved. The deeper they disappeared into the cornfield, the dirt turned to deep pools of mud. They're shoes sank beneath, as if they were walking through quicksand. Tyler's glasses were wet, and he could hardly see. He held onto Ethan's hand, letting him lead the way. Behind him, Tyler held onto Kaitlyn's hand. Walking through the storm was a mission that most would never accomplish.

Kaitlyn wondered if it was dumb to leave the car. Would they have been better off sleeping in the car and waiting until morning to find help? What if no one was in the house she saw? What if the owners were a pair of gun-toting psychopaths? She shook her head. I've been watching too many scary movies.

After an eternity of walking, they escaped the field and found themselves by a small river. Over the river wasn't a house. It was Cedar Creek Grist Mill.

"It's the old Grist Mill," Ethan answered. Tyler shook his head, his eyes wide and his fists in a tight grip. "It's okay, Tyler. It's just a story."

"A story?"

"The town believes the mill is haunted."

Kaitlyn laughed. "Ghosts do not scare me. Let's see if anyone can help us in there."

Tyler didn't want to leave the car, but he also didn't want to be left alone, so he followed the others out of the car. It was a small building with boarded up windows.

Tyler has seen it before on his bicycle. Ever since he was a child, the grist mill sent shivers down his spine. Ethan pushed open the door, and they were met by warmth. A fire was going in an old fireplace.

"Who the Hell are you?"

ONLY TWO HOURS AGO, Jonas Wheeler was preparing for a night out with his beautiful wife and son. It was their anniversary. Twenty-three years of marriage and counting. Jonas stood in his bedroom fixing his tie and putting on his expensive cufflinks. In the bathroom, Barbara Wheeler finished her make-up and tied her long blonde hair up in a neat bun.

"You almost ready?" Jonas called out.

"Yes," she answered. She exited the bathroom in a tight black dress. Her husband grabbed her and kissed her neck.

"You look marvelous."

"Thank you. You don't look so bad yourself," she responded as she ran a finger down his silk tie. She had gotten the tie for him for Christmas. "I'm gonna check on Billy. Once he is ready, we are good to go." As she walked away, Jonas smacked Barb's ass. At fifty-eight years old, she still had a great ass, he thought.

Barb found their twelve-year-old son, William Wheeler, playing Game Boy on his bed. He had on pants and a tee shirt, but no shoes, or tie.

"Billy, we have to go. It's a long drive to the restaurant."

"Just one more round, Mom."

"Now, please. You know how your father gets when he is kept waiting."

Billy sighed and put his toy down. Barb smiled and hugged him. She helped him finish getting ready and tied the tie for him. The boy looked more like his father. He had the same hook nose, the curly brown hair, the thin lips. But he had her blue eyes. The best gift life had given her. He was the making of her and Jonas's love.

Before Billy was born, she doubted herself as a mother. Having her first child at forty-six, she felt that her time had lost. She was divorced with no children, but then she met Jonas at a bar one night and they fell in love instantly, and a year later they were married, and she was pregnant with her first child.

Jonas paced in the kitchen, tapping his foot. He checked his watch. 6:47pm. God Damn it! We should have left fifteen minutes ago!

"Barb! Billy! Time to go," he screamed up the stairs.

Billy ran down the stairs, and Barb helped him into his raincoat. Such an ugly night, she thought. The Wheeler family left their large house and got into the expensive car, Jonas owned. It was his most prized possession, that car. That and his watch. The watch he wore was made of real silver and around the face were diamonds.

The long drive to the restaurant took them out of Raven's Peak, their hometown and through Cedar Creek and into the town after that, Sapphire Meadows. Sapphire Meadows was a well-to-do town and their stood their favorite restaurant. It was the same restaurant Jonas took Barb to propose to all those years ago.

But after dinner, as they drove back home, they got caught in the bad storm in Cedar Creek. A hick town, Jonas always called it. And on the road, outside the grist mill, he had gotten a flat tire. He almost drove off the road. It had come so suddenly. Barb and Billy cried out, and Jonas grabbed the wheel. He didn't want anything to happen to the car. The car was fucking expensive. With an umbrella he stepped out of the car and looked at the damage. Both front tires were torn apart.

"What the fuck," he had said to himself.

He bent down and found barbed wire sitting along the road. Who would have left that out here? It was almost like it was placed deliberately outside the mill.

Barb rolled down the window and asked what was wrong. Jonas stood up and looked his wife in her big round doe-eyes and answered.

"Nothing, just a flat tire. I'm gonna walk into the mill to see if there is a working phone." He couldn't tell his family about the wire. He didn't want to freak them out. He had enough to deal with as is.

Barb opened the door. "We're coming with you then."

She opened the backdoor and Billy got out as well. The rain soaked their bodies, as Jonas kept the umbrella over his head. They walked into the mill and found nothing but garbage and cobwebs. Billy pulled the switch, but no lights came out.

"I don't think they have a phone," the young boy said.

Barb shivered. "There's a fireplace over there. Let's build a fire and wait until the rain lets up."

Jonas nodded. He closed his umbrella and threw loose wood into the fireplace. He poked through his pockets and found a book of matches. He lit a match and threw it into the fireplace. It roared to life as they huddled around the fire. Barb and Billy hugged one another trying to get warm.

Jonas stared at his wife. Her hair was a mess, falling out of the bun, and her mascara ran down her face like black tears. She looks horrible, he thought.

As his family warmed up, Jonas walked towards the boarded up, broken windows and peaked through the cracks as the rain fell. He had a feeling this would be a long night.

TYLER STARED at the family of three that stood by the fire. The older man stood in front of them. The patriarch created a barrier between his wife and child and the strangers. He acted as if this was home and they were the intruders.

"Jonas, please," his wife begged.

"Quiet, Barb. I can handle this. We are in some hick town. They could be dangerous."

Kaitlyn rolled her eyes and walked up to the jerk.

"Listen dude, we just need to get out of the rain."

The older man, Jonas, who didn't want them inside, studied them like insects that needed to be crushed. A shiver ran down Tyler's spine, and when Ethan took his hand, the man's eyes narrowed into slits before he turned his back.

"What's his problem," Ethan whispered into Tyler's ear.

The kind blonde woman shook her head and walked towards their guests. "You all look cold. Come sit by the fire, Dears."

"Barb!"

"Jonas, they're shivering to death." She turned towards the young trio. "Come sit by the fire."

Tyler, Ethan, and Kaitlyn followed the kind woman to the fire and sat down on the floor around it. Tyler wondered why she was with the husband.

"Thank you, ma'am," Ethan responded, letting his southern drawl woo her.

"This is really kind of you," Kaitlyn spoke. The fire was hot on her skin and reminded her of better times. A time when things were simple, and she knew what she wanted in life, but that part of her life was over.

"I'm Barbara Wheeler and this is my son, Billy. That wonderful man who greeted you is my husband, Jonas."

Ethan smiled. He had a smile that could charm anyone. It worked for Tyler at least.

"Nice to meet y'all. I'm Ethan and this is my boyfriend Tyler."

"And I'm Kaitlyn," she threw in. She hated when people introduced her.

Jonas sulked in his wet business suit in the corner. Barb called him over, but he ignored her and stared at the fire. He wasn't going near those hillbilly freaks. He didn't want his son near them either. Those gays might try something on the boy, but Barb was always so damn trusting.

Outside the rain continued on and another bang came at the door.

"You've got to be kidding me. Is this where you people hang out or something?" Jonas said with a bite to his voice.

Everyone ignored him as Ethan opened the door. A young couple stood outside, soaking wet.

"Come in!"

"Thank you," the girl said. The man holding her waist followed her inside. "Our car got a flat outside your place."

"This isn't our place. We were all stranded here too," Kaitlyn answered.

"That's odd," the strange woman said. "By the way, I'm Olivia Mischke, and this is my boyfriend, Jason Palmieri."

Everyone introduced themselves and sat around the fire.

· · ·

Jason and Olivia were from the next town over. They lived together in Raven's Peak. They didn't live in the rich part of town. That was after the railroad tracks, and they lived before it, where all the middleclass people resided. Jason grew up in Cedar Creek, and they were visiting his grandmother. It was supposed to be a simple visit, but the rain made the drive home anything but simple.

And the barbed wire.

Olivia felt like something wasn't right. The barbed wire wasn't just thrown about but looked like it was spread out to catch all the tires on purpose. Jason told her she was overthinking and that it probably fell off someone's truck. She gave in and didn't want to give Jason anymore stress. His grandmother had been sick for a while, and he was her only living relative. His parents died when he was a baby, and he was all the elderly woman had. Olivia knew she would die soon, but Jason didn't want to talk about it. He never wanted to talk about anything meaningful. He'd rather keep everything to himself and that killed her.

But right now, Olivia and Jason were stuck in Cedar Creek in the grist mill that people told stories about. Terrible stories of people going missing and some being found dead. Every town had an urban legend, and Cedar Creek had the Grist Mill. She needed a cigarette badly. She pulled out her cellphone and tried calling for a tow truck, but she couldn't find any service.

Outside of the mill, someone watched. He peaked through the boards over the windows and studied everyone inside. He tilted his head, curious where all the intruders came from. Why were they here? What did they want?

Maybe they were new friends to play with.

TWENTY-TWO

Tyler sat in front of the fire, his head on Ethan's shoulder. Kaitlyn had found an old rocking chair and brought it on over. She closed her eyes and rocked herself. Barb sat on the floor, with her son's head in her lap, while Jason and Olivia searched around the grist mill for anything interesting. Jonas, on the other hand, studied everyone around him. He didn't know any of these people, nor did he trust any of them. Maybe they were the ones who put the barbed wire out there and this was a ruse to get the family alone?

That makes no sense. Why would they crash their own cars? Either way, he would stop at nothing to make sure he and his family make it home okay. Fuck these hicks, he thought.

Jonas pulled out his cellphone and for the tenth time, he tried calling for a tow truck, but he couldn't find a signal. He had service everywhere, but he had to be stranded in the one spot without any.

"Don't bother," Jason said. "Olivia and I have been

trying to call someone. The storm must have knocked something down. We can't get through to anyone."

Jonas said nothing. He answered with a dirty look. He wasn't going to let some idiot tell him what to do. He turned away and dialed the number once more.

"Asshole," Jason muttered.

Olivia giggled and walked over to the fireplace and sat down beside the cute gay couple.

"Tyler, right?"

He looked up and nodded. "And you're Olivia."

She smiled. "How long have you been together?"

Tyler smiled, his face lighting up. Adorable, Olivia thought. "Well we've been best friends all our lives, but we fell in love and we've been together for a few months now."

"Yeah, but it feels like it's been a lifetime," Ethan said, rubbing Tyler's hand in his. "How about you and Jason?"

"Two years, as of yesterday."

"Happy anniversary," Ethan chirped.

"Thanks," she replied. She studied Tyler's face, taking in the bruises and the cuts. She didn't feel those were from their car accident. They looked old, set in. She hoped he was okay. Looking at the blonde boy filled her with a sense of empathy. When she was a little girl, she found a wounded baby owl outside her house. Her father said he should be put out of his misery, but Olivia couldn't let her father do that. She begged her mom to help her save the owl with the broken wing. Together, Olivia and her mom nursed the tiny owl back to health. Olivia cared for the creature and grew to love him, before setting him free. Looking at Tyler now brought back those very same feelings.

"Tyler, you seem like a nice guy. Do you have a lot of friends back home?"

He almost laughed at the question. Instead he shrugged his shoulders. He didn't know how to answer that.

"Not really."

"You seem like a special guy."

"I'm nothing much but thank you."

Olivia grabbed his hand and lifted up his chin. She stared right into his bright blue eyes. Tyler noticed how intense her green eyes were. They were like burning jade.

"Don't say that. You're sweet, attractive, and I've only known you for maybe an hour, but I bet you're funny too."

Ethan smiled. Olivia seemed like a great person, and Tyler needed to hear this.

"I'm really not...I'm nothing to look at. At least not compared to other guys."

"Who says so? Who has called you ugly?"

Once again, Tyler shrugged his shoulders unable to answer another simple question. Why were the simple questions sometimes the hardest to answer? He knew the answer, but he didn't want to say it out loud. Who called him ugly? Mostly himself.

"You're Hollywood ugly."

"Huh?"

"Let me explain. You know how in all those dumb teen movies there some ugly guy is, but he's not really ugly. They always cast the hottest actor to play him. That's you. You're not ugly. You're the hot actor in the glasses who thinks he is."

Tyler smiled. "Thanks, I think. Really, thank you."

Olivia gave him a hug.

"I need a cigarette," Olivia said.

"I thought you're trying to quit," Jason said.

"I am, but this night deserves one." Olivia stood up and walked to the window and looked through the cracks.

"Besides, the rain is starting to slow down. I will stand beneath the awning."

"Be safe."

She laughed. "What's the worst that can happen?"

She stepped outside the mill and pulled out her lighter and cigarettes. She lit one up and sucked in the ashy taste. She listened to the paper fizzle at the end. Music to her ears. Something about the taste felt welcoming. Yeah, it was bad for her, but it was calming for her as well, like a child with a blanket.

She took another drag, before she heard a noise. She looked around the mill but didn't see anyone. It sounded like a heavy footstep on hard wood. She finished her cigarette and stomped it beneath her sneaker.

Smack.

She looked around. She definitely heard something.

"Hello?" she called out. Fucking stupid! This is how those idiots die in those slasher films. She shook her head and turned around, but before she could grab the knob of the door, the Miller jumped from the side of the house and grabbed her. She tried to scream, but he covered her mouth. He lifted his sickle up into the air and brought it down to her neck. Her eyes grew wide and she tried to shake her head. She grabbed onto his arm and pushed, but he was too strong. The rusted blade was at her neck, and soon the Miller dragged the weapon across the flesh, digging in, carving into her neck. He carved into her neck farther and farther, back and forth. Left to right. Her skin tore beneath the blade. She felt every tendon rip and the flesh torn apart. She tried to scream, but all she could do was taste the blood in her throat. She heard herself gasp, a gargling sound in her throat.

Her blood painted the side of the mill, as he pulled the

sickle out and her head fell backwards, still attached to the neck. He had carved halfway through her neck, turning her into a human Pez dispenser.

Rabbitface stared down at the corpse, her blood pooling around her head, staining the wood. With a low growl, he grabbed her by her long red hair and dragged her body away from the mill. Inside, no one suspected a thing, but soon, they would learn about the horror to come.

TWENTY-THREE

Tyler listened to the rain's attack on the roof of the mill. Being inside made him feel uneasy. From the moment he set eyes on it, an ache set root in his stomach. People have disappeared around these parts. A few months ago, he read in the paper about a young woman and her boyfriend going missing. Talia Masters. Tyler saw her sometimes around town. She was older than him. Before he started high school, she had already graduated. Rumors said she was here the night she went missing.

Tyler stood up from beside the fire and walked around the mill. He never took any of it in. Dead animal carcasses littered the floor, some looking like they were eaten raw. On the wall adjacent to the fireplace, was a cider press, an old fashioned one with a metal handle one turned to flatten the apples beneath the press. Tyler saw holes in the walls and some in the wooden floor. As he stepped around, he felt the wood creak, threatening to break beneath his weight any moment. Through a doorway, Tyler entered another room.

The mill was larger than it seemed. Outside the front, it looked like a small box, but inside it was quite vast. Above him was another floor and a ladder stood up against the wall leading up to a trap door above. Another door stood on the wall, leading to the back where the river was. He could see through the window a giant house-sized wooden wheel moving with the water as it flowed through the storm. Tables and chairs stood abandoned in the room, with wooden crates filled with old belongings. Above the table was a wall of farm tools–pitchfork, scythe, corn knife, spade, shovel, trowel, chainsaw, and more. A few spots were empty, he noticed. Tyler peaked through the large crates finding old sunglasses, notebooks, wallets, and other personal belongings. Something was right here. These weren't items people usually left behind. He peaked through the wallets and found them holding cash and credit cards. The IDs were still in place.

What is going on here?

Tyler picked up a woman's wallet and opened it. He gasped dropping the wallet to the floor. They had to get out of here now. Inside the wallet, a photo of a pretty woman with blonde curls smiled up at him.

Talia!

JASON PACED BACK and forth in the other room. Where was Olivia? She should have been back by now? How long did it take to smoke a fucking cigarette? He checked his watch. She had been gone for fifteen minutes now. Barb held Billy in her arms and brushed his hair with her hands, while Jonas eyes the younger man. His constant footsteps back and forth, back and forth, was causing his head to pound.

"Will you stop your damn pacing? It's giving me a migraine!"

"Jonas," Barb hissed.

"I'm worried. Olivia should have been back by now."

"I'm sure she is fine," Kaitlyn said, but how did she know, she thought. This was turning into a strange night.

TYLER WALKED PAST THE LADDER, feeling something wet plop onto his skin. He looked at his hand, finding red. What the fuck! He looked up at the trapdoor and found a red stain pooling over his head. He grabbed onto the ladder and put a foot on the first step. The stench that emerged nearly made him lose his footing. It smelled of something rotten. Almost like rotten eggs or spoiled milk. Possibly worse. His stomach felt almost empty as he began his ascent up the ladder.

JASON HAD ENOUGH. He was going out to find his girlfriend. He pulled zipped up his hoodie and grabbed the door.

"Where are you going?" Barb asked.

"To find Olivia. I will be right back."

He closed the door and walked out into the pouring rain. Outside the rain was coming down fast but was beginning to show signs of slowing down. He pulled up his hood and called out Olivia's name. Where was she? This wasn't like her to just disappear.

FLIES BUZZED around above Tyler's head. What was up there? A dead animal? It surely smelled like it. He's seen enough dead animals to know the smell. It was ingrained in his brain, carved there. It wasn't a large ladder, but the smell was holding him back, like a wall.

·　·　·

OUTSIDE, Jason called out his girlfriend's name. Where the hell was she? He stepped out from the awning and walked around the house and screamed. Inside the scream was heard. Tyler jumped off the ladder and ran into the next room.

"What was that?"

"Jason. He went outside to find Olivia."

Everyone stood by the fire, wondering why he screamed. Tyler thought at that very moment, all the stories are true. This place is haunted.

"Screw this, I'm going to see what's going on," Jonas said.

"Be careful," Barb worried.

He rolled his eyes and walked out of the door. Outside he saw only darkness and heard the rain. He walked around the grist mill, finding Jason on the ground.

"Kid, you okay?"

The boy didn't move.

"Kid, you hear me?"

Jonas walked up to Jason and nearly fell at the sight of him holding his dead girlfriend. He was covered in her blood.

"You're fucking psycho!"

Jonas stood up and ran back inside. Jason ran after him screaming. Everyone inside gasped at the sight of the bloody Jason.

"The kid is crazy! He killed that girl!"

"I didn't kill her. I love her. I found her that way."

"Then who killed her?" Jonas pushed on.

Jason closed his eyes and tried to hold back his tears. "I don't know. She was on the ground like that."

He took a step forward, but they all moved backwards.

"Why are you all so afraid? I didn't kill her, I swear!"

He reached for Tyler's arm, grabbing it. He looked into the boy's eyes and pleaded. Tyler stood still, frozen in the spot. He never saw Ethan grab a shovel, nor did he see Ethan smash the tool over his head. Jason fell to the ground, and Tyler came to. He looked up to see Ethan throw down the shovel. He ran to Tyler and pulled him in a hug.

"Are you okay?"

"Yeah, I'm fine. Thank you."

"What do we do now?" Billy asked.

Barb grabbed her son and held him close.

"We'll be okay, Honey."

"We should tie him up, just in case."

Jonas looked at Kaitlyn and laughed. "That's a brilliant idea. He could get loose and kill us too. We should just kill him now."

"Are you fucking crazy," she spit. "We don't know anything. He could be telling the truth."

"No one was fucking out there! There was no psycho in a mask. This isn't a movie. That guy over there went crazy and brutally murdered his innocent girlfriend. These kinds of crimes happen all the time in the world."

"Crimes of passion," Barb muttered. He had a point, but she didn't think it was right. Something wasn't clicking for her. If he truly killed his girlfriend, then where was his weapon? Why didn't he attack them? And his eyes. She looked into his brown eyes and saw nothing but fear. No anger. Just cold-blooded fear. "I think he is telling the truth."

Jonas looked at his wife and raised an eyebrow.

"Honey, stay out of this. I know what I'm doing. You boys, look for rope. Brunette girl, do something."

"We have names," Ethan said.

"I don't care."

"Jonas, you're being an asshole," his wife spoke up. She was starting to have enough of his shit. They were all in the same situation. They should be working together, not fighting, but Jonas seemed to be splitting them apart at the very seems.

Her husband turned and glared at her. She took a step back, pushing Billy behind her body. Why did I do that? She didn't believe he'd ever harm her or her son, but something in his eyes told her to stand between him and her son.

"Barb, please shut up!"

Barb nodded and hugged Billy close. Billy was young but he thought as his mother held him, that he'll never in his life act like his father.

Kaitlyn shook her head and followed Tyler and Ethan to the other room. They dug through the crates and bins, until they found rope.

"That guy is a real asshole. I feel bad for his poor wife and son."

"Yeah, and that girl. Olivia. Do you think Jason really killed his girlfriend," Ethan asked.

Tyler shook his head. "I think he is being honest."

"It looked like he was about to attack you," Ethan said.

"I don't think he was. I think he was just scared."

Ethan shrugged his shoulders, as Kaitlyn looked between the two young men. She didn't know what to think. She didn't see the girl's body. Maybe he did kill his girlfriend. Maybe he didn't. It was better to be safe, than sorry. But if he didn't kill her...then that would mean they weren't alone.

TWENTY-FOUR

A hammer-like throbbing pierced his head, as Jason woke up. What the fuck happened? Did he have a nightmare? Why couldn't he move? He opened his eyes and saw everyone staring at him. It wasn't a dream. It was real. Olivia was dead. And they were trapped. He looked down at himself, finding his hands tied behind his back to an old radiator.

"What the fuck!"

"Don't move," Jonas warned him.

"Where the fuck am I going to move to? You tied me up! Untie me! I didn't kill her. I swear. Someone is out there."

"Oh yeah, who?"

Jason shook his head. "I don't know. I didn't see anyone. But when I went out there, Olivia was on the ground with her head nearly sliced off. How could I have done that, Jonas? I have no weapons on me? You think about that, asshole?"

Jonas stayed silent. Ethan thought about that. He was right. Even if he did have a weapon, nothing he'd be able to hide in his pocket could do the damage he was talking about.

Olivia's corpse sunk into the mud as the rain came to an end. Rabbitface looked over at her. He sniffed her neck, taking in the light notes of her perfume and the aroma that radiated off a woman. He grabbed her auburn hair and pulled it to his nose, breathing her in. He lunged at the mill, looking through the windows at the people inside his home. His eyes focused on the blonde boy with the glasses, as he became erect, the Miller shoved a free hand down his pants and masturbated. That boy could stay here in the mill with him forever.

Friend, he thought.

Tyler shivered by the fire. Ethan sat down and put an arm around him. He rubbed circles onto his back and let him rest his head on his shoulder. When they sat down, they were closer in height, and Ethan loved that.

"What do you think should be the first thing we do when we get to California?" Ethan asked.

Tyler thought about it. All he could think about was that poor dead girl. How could he think about anything else?

"I don't know," he answered. "What about you?"

Ethan wanted to get Tyler's mind off of everything going on. But how could he with all that has been happening in the past few days, and now this?

"Find a home for us. Not just a house, but our very own home."

Tyler smiled. "I'm going to say that too."

"Favorite color?" Ethan asked.

"You know it's blue."

Ethan gave him a small smile, "I know. I'm just trying to get your mind to focus on other things."

Tyler kissed him and hugged him close. He breathed in his natural musk and closed his eyes. He rested his head on his chest and wrapped his arms tight around Ethan's waist.

"I appreciate that, but nothing will help right now. A girl is dead."

"I know. Jason…"

"No! It wasn't Jason. There is someone out there."

"Tyler, how can that be?"

"Listen to me." Tyler pulled away and looked right into Ethan's eyes. "I looked into Jason's eyes. He was scared to death. He was telling us the truth, and back at the car I saw someone in the cornfield. I told you guys that, but neither of you believed me. Someone is out there. We are not alone."

Kaitlyn sat down with the boys, thinking that Tyler might be right. What if Jason didn't kill his girlfriend? If that was true, then they weren't alone.

"You really did see someone out there, didn't you?" she asked.

"Yes, I did. We aren't alone here. We need to get out of here."

"And go where?" she asked.

She had a point, Tyler thought. Where could they go. Back to the car where they were stuck? Into the woods or the cornfields with no protection? Their best chance was to stay put in the mill. There were two entrances. One in the front, and one in the back. If they could barricade the doors, they could be okay? Nearly all the windows were boarded up. All except one large window in the main room by the fireplace. Tyler stood up and searched the room, finding broken chairs and loose wood.

"What are you doing?" Jonas asked.

"We need to barricade the doors and windows, if we want to be okay. I saw a hammer and nails in the next room with the tools."

"Are you fucking stupid? The killer is right here?"

Jason rolled his eyes. "Fuck off!"

Jonas said nothing.

"And if you're wrong," Tyler defiantly said, standing his ground. He stared straight into Jonas's eyes and didn't waver. His back was straight, and his hands were clenched in fists at his sides. Ethan had never seen him so strong-willed and confident before. Something in him was changing. He was always strong. Stronger, than Tyler gave himself credit for.

"I'm not wrong." Jonas checked his watch. When would they get out of here?

"Stop looking at your damn watch and listen to me," Tyler barked. Everyone stopped and looked at the wide-eyed boy. Even he seemed surprised by his own order.

"Listen, boy. Don't tell me what to do. This watch is worth more than your entire life. So, sit down, and shut the fuck up. You hear me?"

Tyler said nothing. He stood silent and turned away. He had enough talking to the asshole. He walked into the next room and grabbed the hammer from the wall and opened a drawer, finding a box of nails. He walked back to the main room.

Ethan and Kaitlyn walked to his side. They would help him.

"Boy, what the hell are you doing?"

"I already told you, boy. I'm going to make this place safe."

"And we are going to help him," Ethan backed him up. Tyler grabbed his hand and smiled at his boyfriend. Goddamn, he loved him so much.

Together three of them went about boarding up the doors and the bare windows. Jonas watched with an incredulous smirk. Fucking idiots, he thought. They had the killer tied up right here.

Barb stood up and walked after them.

"What do you think you're doing?"

"I'm going to help them."

"Are you serious? Sit down, Barbara!"

"I love you, Jonas. I really do, but I can't stand by you and let this go on. I'm doing this to protect ourselves and our son."

"Barb, get back here!"

She walked towards the others and grabbed a hammer and part of a table they had ripped apart. Ethan smiled at her.

"I'm glad you came to help."

"Me too."

While his wife helped the fucking idiots, Jonas sat beside the fire and watched the prisoner stare at them.

"What are you looking at?"

"You're making a huge mistake. Someone is out there. Sooner or later he will get in. You need to untie me, so I can help make this place safe."

"No one is getting in. You killed her. Your own damn girlfriend. Pathetic."

Jason shook his head. This was a losing battle. He looked at the kid sitting beside his father. He looked like a nice boy. Billy, he thought his name was. He hoped he turned out more like his mother than his father. He was young enough to choose his own path.

Outside, the Miller watched from his seat on the ground as the strangers ran about his home, playing with the boards. With his head tilted to the side and confusion on his mind, he watched them. He saw the blonde boy with a hammer, nailing part of a table to the door. He couldn't wait to get inside and play with his new friends.

CHAPTER
TWENTY-FIVE

Tyler looked around the mill. It was nearly a fortress. He wasn't feeling safe, but this was a step in the right direction. He knew it was idiotic to think they could stay here, but eventually they would have to deal with the outside threat. Outside the rain had ended. All they heard was the slight dripping of water from the trees onto the roof. When the sun came up, they could all get out of here. But how exactly would they drive away in the car that lied dead in a ditch.

Only one window remained clear. It was a large window, and nothing was big enough to cover it. It overlooked the dirt road in the front and gave Tyler a perfect view of the cornfield and the scarecrow that stood not too far away.

"You okay?"

Ethan wrapped his arms around Tyler's waist and snuggled into his back. The top of his head came up to his shoulders. Tyler turned around and hugged him back. He rested his head on top of Ethan's.

"Yeah, I'm just thinking."

"About what?"

"Do you think we will make it out of here okay? Be honest."

"Yes, I do. I will make sure we do. You and I will get out of this, together. I promise, Tyler."

Tyler bent down and kissed Ethan on the lips, giggling as Ethan nibbled on his bottom lip. Tyler had to admit that felt good. They would have to do that more often after they get out of this alive. In one another's arms, they always found happiness; they didn't notice the sneer that sat on Jonas's face. Disgusting, he thought. If Billy ended up being like that, I'd kick him out of the house. Barb smiled at the young lovers, while Kaitlyn rested her back against the wall with her eyes closed.

Billy watched the window. He missed his bed. He let out a yawn, wishing he was home. What if this was God's way of punishing him for not always being a good boy? Was this his fault? The church always said God would punish naughty children and sometimes he fought against his parents. He was on his Gameboy too often and sometimes would skip brushing his teeth before bed. God, I promise to always listen to my parents and be good from now on.

As the young boy prayed, he saw a flash pass before the window. His eyes grew wide and his jaw fell open. He tried to talk, but nothing came out. His vocal chords were frozen. He began to shake in his spot on the floor. There was someone out there. No, not a person. It was a monster. A scream erupted from his body.

Everyone turned towards the boy and Barb ran to her son and hugged him close.

"What's wrong? Billy, what's wrong?"

"I saw something! There was a monster outside!"

"A monster?" Barb asked.

"Yes! He was hideous."

Jonas growled. "Look what everyone did to him! You all scared him and now he thinks he saw a monster."

"I don't think so. I definitely saw a monster, Dad! He was outside the window. I swear!"

Jonas shook his head. What the fuck was the kid going on about? He watched the window, and nothing was there. Barb stood up and walked towards the window.

"Barb, sit down."

"Stop telling me to sit down," she told her husband. She looked at her son and smiled. Her smile was the kind that only a mother wore for their child. "I'm going to look outside the window, okay Billy?"

The boy shook his head. "Mommy, don't! Please, come back."

"It'll be okay!"

Barb's heart pounded within her chest. She hoped it would be okay at least. She couldn't show her son her fear. He needed to believe in her. She needed to be his protector. She was Mother Hen, and no one was going to get her chick. Kaitlyn stood up as well and walked up to the window. The foursome stared outside, but only saw the night. The clouds were dissipating, and the light of the moon was beginning to shine down, casting a spotlight on the scarecrow.

"At least the rain stopped," Kaitlyn said. She wished she had her camera. Sometimes that was the only thing that could calm her down. All she needed was to hold it. Feel the metal in her hands. Smell the film inside. Children had blankets for security; she had a camera.

Barb peered outside the window but saw nothing. She turned around and looked at Billy.

"It's okay. Nothing is out there."

Glass shattered, and screams penetrated the silence. Billy yelled out for his Mommy, while Jonas jumped up and pushed the others out of his way. It was too late, when he got to the window. Tyler held onto Ethan's arms, staring in shock. Kaitlyn screamed.

Barb never saw the Miller break through the window. His hands grabbed her by the neck and lifted her out through the window. They all saw the hideous mask he wore. The dead rabbit's face. The dirty floppy ears. The barbed wire that held it to his head. Blood dripped down his face from the little holes the wire left behind.

Jonas jumped through the window and ran after his wife, whose screams left a trail of breadcrumbs for him. He followed her shrieks and yelled out for Barb. He had to get to her. Time was running out. Everything those kids said was true. Fuck!

The Miller ran into the cornfield. Jonas continued to run after them. He had to catch up. He needed to get to his wife. He screamed out her name and found the ugly fucker stop. He held Barb's hair in his hand and turned around. He tilted his head and watched Jonas. In his other hand, he held his sickle.

"Leave her alone!"

Barb cried and fought at the asshole's hand. She dug her nails into his hand, but it didn't seem to even feel the pain. He threw Barb to the ground and she closed her eyes as she lifted herself up. Jonas opened his arms, but before Barb could run, the Miller brought the sickle down into her shoulder.

"No!"

He grabbed the top of her head and ripped the sickle out and Jonas watched as the monster ripped his weapon out and brought it back down into her shoulder, deeper than before. Further into her chest. She screamed out in agony as the pain erupted in her body. Jonas couldn't move. All he could do was stare as his wife was hacked away by the Rabbit-faced motherfucker. Blood dripped from her mouth as the sickle reached her chest.

"Fuck!"

Jonas ran back away, back towards the grist mill. The sickle reached her heart and part of her body fell off, hanging by the skin. Her should and arm dangled at her side as Rabbitface threw her corpse down. He ran after the new widower.

Jonas screamed out as he ran back for the mill. He didn't dare turn around, afraid the asshole would be behind him. He screamed out for help. The Miller followed after him. Jonas ran up to the Miller and slammed his whole body against the door.

"Let me in! Please! Help!"

He turned around and saw the Miller walk out of the cornfield. His wife's blood dripped from the sickle. No!

"We can't get the door open! Go back through the window!"

Jonas couldn't hear a word. All he could listen to, was the beating of his heart. His focus was on the Miller walking towards him. He screamed. He didn't want to die. He couldn't die like this. He wasn't an animal.

As the Miller walked closer and closer, Jonas took notice of the window and ran towards it. He took off his blazer and wrapped his hands inside the jacket and knocked all the jagged glass from the windowpane. He threw the jacket down and crawled inside.

He screamed as Rabbitface grabbed his foot.

"Help!"

Kaitlyn and Ethan ran and grabbed his hands. Tyler

held onto Billy. The Miller's grasp on the man's ankle was hard. Ethan and Kaitlyn had to fight to keep a hold on him.

"I don't want to die!"

The Miller lifted up his weapon and brought it down into his leg. Jonas screamed at the avalanche of pain. As the Miller ripped the sickle out, Ethan and Kaitlyn pulled Jonas inside. They all stepped away from the window and watched as the Miller stared them each down one by one. He was studying them. Kaitlyn felt like the spider that was in her sink and this was the sink.

"Fuck you," she screamed.

"Get me out of here!" Jason screamed.

Tyler got down on his knees and looked at the knots. Jonas tied them tight. Tyler couldn't figure out where the knots even began.

"Shit!"

"Don't say that, Tyler. That means something bad is happening."

"I've got this," Tyler reassured him.

Billy ran to his father and hugged him, crying into his shoulder.

"Where is Mommy?"

Jonas said nothing. He hugged his son and let him cry. He couldn't bring himself to say it out loud. He let her down. She was dead, and he couldn't get to her in time. He and Billy had to get out of here, no matter what. Fuck these people. He didn't give a damn. It was their fault they were in this situation. It was only about he and Billy surviving now.

TWENTY-SIX

It was silent outside the grist mill. The only sounds were the hammers in Kaitlyn and Ethan's hands as they nailed a table to the open window. Tyler went through the bins looking for anything useful. He saw into the Miller's eyes and there was nothing behind them. People had a soul in their eyes, and the masked man had nothing. His eyes were blank. He needed a bigger weapon.

Ethan entered the room and grabbed his shoulder. Tyler jumped, spinning around.

"Sorry, what are you doing back here?"

"That guy outside...did you see his eyes? They were the devil's eyes, Ethan. We need better protection. The barricade isn't going to hold for much longer."

"He's only a man. He bleeds just like anyone else."

"He already killed Barb and Olivia. Who will be next? What if it is you? Ethan, what if he gets you next?"

He pulled Tyler into a hug, wrapping his arms around his waist. He crushed the boy to his body and rubbed the back of his head, letting his fingers tangle in his blonde hair.

"He's not, I promise. You and I will be okay. We are going to get out of here and live our life together. I told you."

Tyler nodded, his body shaking. The rabbit-faced man outside was a psycho. He didn't care about the promise Ethan had made him. If he lost Ethan, he would give up and die. He was the reason he was still going. He saved him every day of his life, and now as he looked down upon his beautiful face, he knew it was time for him to save Ethan.

They turned towards the wall of weapons. Ethan lifted the axe off the wall and held it in his hands. It was heavy in his hands but had a good weight to swing. Ethan smiled at his boyfriend. They'll be okay. The Miller had a sickle and now he was armed with a large axe. He could take him.

"I love you," Ethan stated.

"I love you too."

The Miller stalked the outside of the grist mill. There were other ways inside. Inside the intruders thought they blocked all the ways inside, but Rabbitface loved the game they were playing. He grabbed onto the side of the mill, stabbing his sickle into the wood. Above on the second floor was an opened window. The Miller smiled as he ascended the side of the mill like it was Mount Everest. He would be in soon enough, and then the fun would really begin.

Inside the main room, Kaitlyn worked on the knots behind Jason's back. She was frustrated. He was bound so tight, she didn't know how long it would take her to get him loose.

"How's it going back there, Katie?"

"It won't be good if you called me Katie again."

"Duly noted. How's it going, Kaitlyn?"

"I'm trying. At this rate, I should have you untied by tomorrow evening."

Jason groaned. He couldn't stand being tied up any longer. There was a sicko outside with a weapon and he was waiting to get in and make mincemeat of them all.

"Please, hurry up. I don't want to die here."

"You won't die here."

"Promise?"

Kaitlyn remained silent. How could she answer that? She didn't know. He might in fact die in the mill tonight. Hell, they might all die inside here tonight. The future was uncertain, and Kaitlyn couldn't give him false hope.

"I will try my best."

"That doesn't sound hopeful."

Jonas didn't care about the girl or the ropes. They could stay here and rot, but he and Billy would be okay. He sat by the fire, staring at the boarded-up window. His leg was wrapped up with the arm of his blazer. Billy sat behind him. Barb was dead. His beautiful wife was ripped apart before his very own eyes and he felt nothing but rage boiling inside his body. His blood was hot, and his mind was waiting to explode. He needed to get out of there. He could no longer stay trapped inside the fucking mill.

"Aren't there tools in the next room? Maybe there is something sharp to cut the ropes," Jason said.

Fuck! Why didn't I think of that, Kaitlyn thought. Her mind had been all over the place. She jumped up and ran into the next room to find Tyler and Ethan still inside. She studied the wall of tools.

Creeeeeeeak...

"What was that?" she asked.

"I don't know," Ethan said. "But it came from above."

The three of them stared at the ladder and the door above where the foul stench came from. Ethan lifted up his axe, while Tyler grabbed a flashlight from the work bench. It still worked. He turned it on and grabbed onto the ladder.

"Be careful," Kaitlyn said.

Tyler nodded and covered his nose and mouth with his sweater. He pushed open the trap door and gagged at the horrible smell. He looked around with the flashlight and let out a short shriek. Inside were the bodies of Talia and her father, and so many more. Faces from missing posters he had seen over the years posted all over the town. Most were decomposing, while some were nothing but bones and dust. Maggots crawled out of their wounds.

"What is going on?" Ethan demanded.

"It's nothing. No one is up here."

But what made the creaking noise then? Ethan stared up at Tyler and screamed as a pair of hands grabbed onto his neck. The flashlight fell to the ground, the glass shattering. Ethan climbed up the ladder and tried to hit the Miller's arm with the axe, but the asshole was too swift. He let go of Tyler's neck.

Tyler fell down the ladder, tumbling onto Ethan. The axe slid across the floor. The Miller jumped down from above landing on his feet. His back was hunched as he looked at the three of them. Tyler stared right into his eyes, but this time they weren't blank. They looked like a child's eyes. Almost innocent.

The Miller lunged at the boys and Ethan pulled Tyler out of the way. Kaitlyn helped them up and they ran into the next room. The Miller chased after them. Everyone screamed as Jonas lifted up Billy. He ran to the door and tried to pull off the boards.

"God damn it!" he screamed. They locked themselves inside with the monster.

As Jonas tried to pull at the boards, Kaitlyn ran to help. Tyler dived for Jason's wrists, pulling at the ropes. Jason screamed and cried. He couldn't be trapped like this. He couldn't die like an animal awaiting slaughter. Sweat soaked Tyler's hands. Oh God, he was going to let Jason die.

Ethan grabbed a wooden beam and swung it before him. The Miller held the axe. He watched Ethan as he kept swinging the large beam.

Ethan swore he looked amused. He cursed him to leave them alone.

Jonas and Kaitlyn pulled off one wooden beam.

"Hurry, Daddy!"

Billy shrieked as he watched the other boy defend himself against the monster. Ethan ran for the miller, swinging the board across his head. The Miller went down, and Ethan brought the heavy wood down again.

Another wooden beam ripped off the door. One more to go.

Tyler opened one knot, but there were still so many to go.

"Please hurry, Tyler. I don't want to die," he blubbered. Tyler said nothing. All he could do was focus on the ropes, but he couldn't stop his eyes moving towards Ethan, who brought the wooden beam down once again.

Jonah and Kaitlyn ripped off the final board on the entrance. Jonah grabbed his son and pushed Kaitlyn aside, running out the door.

"Asshole," she screamed!

"Kaitlyn, go!" Ethan screamed!

She stood there frozen. Could she really leave them? Her new friends, she just met. She took one look at the monster's rabbit face, and at the three men. She wanted to run. Her legs begged her to run. Her brain yelled for survival, but her heart made her stay. She ran to Tyler's side and tried to help with Jason's ropes.

The Miller grabbed Ethan by the throat and threw him against the wall. The boy cried as pain erupted through his back. It vibrated through his spine like a xylophone.

"Ethan!"

Tyler grabbed the wooden beam and ran, swinging the beam. It splintered across the Miller's back. The Miller turned around and swung the sickle. Tyler tried to move, but the blade dug into his bicep, tearing through the cloth of this shirts. Tyler screamed, falling back onto his butt. Ethan jumped up and threw his weight against the masked psycho. Tyler grabbed the beam again, and once more slammed it with all of his strength over their attacker's head. The board broke in half and he went down. Tyler threw his wooden weapon onto the floor and grabbed onto his arm, gasping. Ethan ran to his side and hugged him. Tyler wanted to be held in Ethan's arms, but Jason's whimpers were the reality he had to face.

"I can't get him untied," Kaitlyn screamed.

THE MILLER STOOD up and grabbed his sickle. His disgusting rabbit face stared at the four young adults. Ethan grabbed onto the ropes and pulled.

"Please, hurry," Jason blubbered. He didn't want to die. Not yet. Not here.

"Shit!" Ethan barked.

The Miller ran towards them, lifting his sickle up in the air. He brought it down. Blood splattered Tyler's face. He and Kaitlyn jumped back. The sickle stuck out of Jason's head. The rounded blade came out of his eye socket. Jason's hazel eye sat on the tip of the blade. His other eye twitched as his body shook.

Tyler sat there frozen. He brought his hand to his face and stared down at the blood that was not his own. Tyler looked from his hand up at the Miller's face. Beneath the mask he saw the eyes of the Devil.

Ethan pulled at Tyler's wrist, but all Tyler could do was stare at the monster. He willed his body to move but the neurons in his brain were cut off.

The Miller ripped out the sickle, the eyeball falling to the floor. Beneath his heavy boot, the Miller's foot crushed the eyeball. Like a large but, it gave off a gooey squish. The sound brought Tyler out of his daze. Kaitlyn and Ethan help him up, breaking the connection between Tyler and the Miller. The killer tilted his head as he looked at Tyler. Tyler grabbed onto his bicep pulsating with blood.

Ethan wrapped an around Tyler's waist and helped Kaitlyn out of the door. She ran straight for the trees. The Miller grabbed Tyler's shirt collar and pulled him back inside. Ethan spun around and screamed. He charged, throwing his entire body at the Miller.

"Tyler, run!"

Tyler jumped up. He stared at the opened door and at Ethan was fighting Rabbitface. He shook his head and ran into the next room. He looked at the wall of tools and grabbed the machete off the wall.

The Miller grabbed Ethan by the neck and lifted him into the air. Ethan scratched at the killer's hands. His grasp was so tight. It felt like his neck was being crushed. He tried to breathe, but all he could do was gasp. He was going to die, but all he could think about was Tyler. Tyler had to get out of here.

Tyler ran back into the room and swung the machete. The long blade sliced open the Miller's back. A wolf-like howl escaped his mouth. He let go and Ethan fell to the floor, choking for air. He looked at Tyler holding the bloody weapon. Behind his glasses, his eyes were wide and full of shock. Ethan just saw sweet innocent Tyler stab another person.

Tyler looked down at his bloody hands and the weapon he held. Did he really do that?

Ethan grabbed Tyler's hand and lead him outside. It was time to go! Ethan slammed the door shut and turned to Tyler.

"Hey, Tyler, it's okay." He took the machete from his lover's hand and kissed him. "Let's go."

Ethan let go and started to run towards the woods. Tyler ran after, but before he could react, a hand grabbed his hair and covered his mouth and he was pulled back towards the grist mill. Ethan disappeared among the dark trees.

TWENTY-SEVEN

"Tyler, how are you holding up?"

Ethan was met by nothing but silence. He turned around and brought a hand to his mouth. Where was he?

"Tyler," he shouted.

Fuck! What happened? He was right behind him. He spun around looking in every direction, hoping that Tyler would suddenly appear like a ghost. He promised Tyler he'd protect him, and he failed. He failed the love of his life.

In the brush he heard a crunch of a twig.

"Tyler," he whispered, his voice stuck in his throat. He held the machete up and walked towards the noise.

"Watch it!"

Jonas dragged Billy out from beyond the trees. Tears ran down the child's face.

"Where are Tyler and Kaitlyn?"

"How am I supposed to know? Can you please lower that?"

Ethan lowered his machete. Did Tyler get lost in the

woods? Was he too fast for him? Or…did the fucker get him…

No! He couldn't think like that. Tyler was alive, and he'd find him and get him out of here.

"My car isn't far off, I think. Come on!"

"I am not going without the others. We can't leave Tyler and Kaitlyn behind."

Jonas scoffed, shaking his head. "Kid, I'm not waiting around for your little faggot, just so we can get killed."

"Fuck you!"

"No, fuck you! I have my son to worry about. My wife is dead, so excuse me if I don't care. We are going to my car, and you can either come or stay."

Ethan shook his head. He'd rather face the killer than be in a car with Jonas.

"Dad, please stop. We should help him. They're good people. They helped us before."

His father pushed him aside. Billy groaned. Why did his father have to be such a dick all the time? He looked up at Ethan and looked right into his brown eyes. Ethan looked back and felt a world of pain for the kid.

Tyler woke up on the floor of the mill. His ankles and wrists were tied. Blood dripped from his head. The splintering floor dug into his back.

What happened? He tried to sit up, but his head pounded. He looked around the room, finding the Miller on the opposite side by the fireplace. He is watching the flames flicker. Tyler tried to undo the ropes around his wrist, but he couldn't get his fingers in between the bindings. Fuck! He was stuck. He rolled onto his side and saw a large glass shard staring him right in the face. He looked up at the

Miller. He still watched the fire. Tyler rolled over, landing on the glass, grabbing it in his hands. Beneath his back, he twirled the glass like a baton and brought it to the ropes. Back and forth. Back and forth. Like a tiny handsaw, he worked at the ropes.

He looked over at the Miller, who was still watching the flames. He put his hand over the fire and tilted his head to the side. He let the flames burn his hand. He lowered his fingers and with a sharp yelp, he ripped his hand away and held it to his chest.

While the killer was distracted, Tyler continued to saw aw the ropes. The tight ropes bruised his wrists. Like tiny hairs being torn, the glass slowly cut through the ropes. *Come on*, Tyler begged.

The glass slipped from his hands, hitting the wooden floor. The Miller turned towards Tyler. He reached for his sickle and crawled towards his hostage. Tyler flattened his back onto the floor, covering the glass.

Rabbitface studied the boy's boy. He crouched over his intended victim and dragged the blade across his cheek and along his neck. Tyler closed his eyes and bit into his lip. The metal was hot and sticky with blood, threatening to release his. Beneath his back, he grabbed onto the glass and slowly worked on the rope.

The Miller dragged his sickle away from his body. Tyler wanted to let out a sigh of relief, but he forgot how to breathe. All he could see was the disgusting mask and the weapon in his hand. The Miller reached for the boy's face and caressed Tyler's smooth skin. The Miller studied him. Tyler was no more than a science experiment, like a frog waiting to be dissected. The Miller lied his head on Tyler's chest. He listened to the heartbeat as blood pumped through his body.

Tyler quickened his speed and got farther through the rope. The Miller lifted up his head and stood up. Tears welled up in Tyler's eyes. He felt naked as the monster analyzed him. The Miller grabbed his sickle and walked away into the next room. Tyler sat up and sawed through the ropes as fast as he could. Like wild animal he moved the glass. Come on! The rope broke freeing his purple wrists. He had no time to think about the pain. He dug the glass into the rope around his ankles. Little by little it tore.

Almost there!

Halfway through the rope. Not too much more.

Almost free.

Footsteps echoed as the Miller entered the room. Tyler fell onto his back, placing his hands behind his body. The Miller watched the boy. Tyler could tell by the tilt of the fucker's head, he knew something was wrong. The Miller walked towards him, like a bear on his hind legs. He bent down over Tyler and ran his hand up Tyler's leg. Tyler shivered at the touch. It was acid to his body. He needed a shower.

The Miller pushed his hand beneath Tyler's button-up shirt, feeling the smooth tense muscles of his stomach. Tyler tried not to cry, but he couldn't help the screech that escaped his mouth. The Miller moved his hand up to Tyler's chest. His nails were dirty and sharp. They dug into his flesh.

The Miller's other hand felt his leg and moved upwards to his crotch. Tyler cried out as the killer groped the bulge inside his khakis.

No more!

Tyler say up and screamed, digging the glass right into the Miller's left eye. The monster screamed and ran around the room clutching his eye. Tyler grabbed onto the rope around his ankles and pulled. They nearly fell apart.

He looked up at the Miller who slammed his body at the wall. Angrier and angrier he grew.

With one more tug, Tyler ripped the rope off his leg. He stood up and ran for the door. With one last look back, he stared at the Miller, who looked back with his one eye. The Miller grabbed his sickle and Tyler ran. He ran as fast as his legs could take him. It was about survival now, but first he must find Ethan.

Kaitlyn wondered the woods alone. Looking around, where should she go? She leaned up against a tree. She had to catch her breathe. If she ran anymore, her lungs would give out or she'd die of a heart attack. Her lungs were on fire. What would kill her first? The asshole in the mask, or her own body's betrayal. She was fucked.

She was fucked, and she was along. All she saw were trees everywhere. Each one looked the same to her. Where was she to go? Even if she made it back to the car, it was still not going anywhere. She only had one spare tire and it couldn't exactly fix her car when its wrapped around a tree.

Three people were dead. Who cared about the car? Three innocent people. Yes, they were strangers, but her heart still broke for them. Why did she go this route? Why did she go on this trip? Was this the universe's way of punishing them? Or were dead and this was Hell? They died when they hit that tree. That couldn't be true. She knew it couldn't be, but in her head anything could be possible.

There was so much she wanted to do. SO many things she needed to shoot. So much beauty in the world she wanted to capture and record to memory.

Was life truly this cruel?

Kaitlyn sat down on the grass and closed her eyes. She wanted to sleep. Close her eyes and drift away.

Crunch!

Kaitlyn jumped up at the sound of the crushed twig. Barely a hum, yet it sounded like the crash of a tree to her ears. While her lungs burned, she forced herself to stand up and move. She continued to run, hoping her heart wouldn't give out on her.

Jonas and Billy pushed the branches aside, coming to the same spot, Kaitlyn was at only seconds ago. Ethan followed after, machete still in hand. Ethan didn't want to leave the boy alone with his father, but he was desperate to find Tyler. Every second longer he was away from him, the heavier his heart grew. Becoming a weight, he was forced to carry around.

"Dad, my legs hurt. Can we take a break?"

"No, we have to keep going," his father answered, with even looking at the boy.

"But Dad," he whined.

His father turned around and screamed, "Shut up!"

Ethan jumped at the burst of anger.

"Billy looks exhausted. We can stop for a moment to rest. We've been running for a while it seems."

Jonas did not answer. He turned around and glared at the young man.

"Don't tell me what to do. I know how to raise my son. I'm not going to stop here to die. We need to keep moving."

Before Ethan could say what was on his mind, they grew silent at the sound of trees rustling. All the hatred Ethan felt for the man left in the instant.

"What was that?" Billy asked.

Ethan brought a finger to his pursed lips. Billy nodded.

They watched a bush move. Billy squeaked, and Jonas ripped the machete from Ethan's grip. He held it up.

"Get out of here!" the older man yelled.

As the bush rustled once more, Jonas slowly walked up to the leaves. Something was over there. There was no wind to blame. No imagination going wild. There was something inside the bush. Jonas took a deep breath and tried not to show how fast his heart raced. His hand shook as he reached out and moved the leaves aside.

A possum shrieked at him. He let go of the leaves and lowered his machete with a laugh.

"What is it?" Ethan asked.

"It's a fucking possum!"

Billy grabbed onto Ethan's waist and hugged him tight. Ethan let out a sigh and rubbed the boy's head, ruffling his hair. Jonas felt the disgust in his throat. He didn't want the fag to touch his son.

"Take your hands off of him!"

"Dad..."

"Get away from him, Billy."

As Jonas focused his hate-filled eyes on Ethan, behind him the Miller appeared out of the darkness. Billy screamed, and Jonas turned around. Jonas lifted his machete, but the Miller grabbed his wrist. Billy watched as his father cried out. The machete fell to the ground.

"Dad!"

Jonas couldn't move. He couldn't speak. His body shook. He couldn't reach for the machete. The Miller let go of his wrist and Jonas fell back onto his ass. He shook his head and cried, backing away as the Miller walked after him. Ethan ran toward the older man and helped him up. The Miller watched the two men and moved his focus. Jonas followed the fucker's gaze as it landed on his son.

Billy stood to the side frozen in fear, mouth wide open with no sound coming out.

"Billy, run!" Ethan screamed.

The Miller walked towards the young boy. Jonas had to do something. He had to stop him! Billy wouldn't move. Why wouldn't he just run? The Miller towered over the boy. He held the sickle at his side and stared at Billy. He tilted his head to the side. Billy stared up into the one angry eye. The other was a bloody mess.

"Please don't hurt me," Billy begged.

The Miller raised his sickle and Jonas screamed.

"I have to protect my son!" Jonas grabbed onto Ethan.

"What the fuck are you doing, you crazy bastard?"

Jonas pushed him, but Ethan grabbed onto the watch. The watch slipped off his wrist and Ethan fell towards the Miller.

It happened in slow motion for Billy. Ethan fell into the Miller's body. He didn't even feel his father grab his shoulders to pull him away. Ethan screamed, but Billy could not hear the words he was saying. The world was put on mute. Ethan tried to fight off the Miller but gasped as the sickle entered his stomach.

All sound came back, and Billy screamed for the young man who had protected him tonight. Jonas dragged Billy away. Billy looked up at his father as they ran. He felt like a void. His father killed that man. He killed Ethan. His father was a murderer. He is no better than the monster who killed Mommy.

After escaping, Billy ripped his wrist out of his father's hands and stopped running. He couldn't hide the disgust from his eyes.

"What?"

Billy's mouth was agape, and his eyes were wide.

"You killed him."

"I was protecting you, Billy."

The boy shook his head, taking a step back from his father. Jonas reached out for his son, but Billy jumped back.

"Don't touch me!

"Billy?"

"No! You're a killer. Like that man in the mask."

Jonas shook his head. That wasn't true. He did what he had to do. He was only trying to save his son. Billy would understand one day. He was only a child. He didn't know how the world worked. Jonas knew how ruthless it was and how to survive. In order to survive, you must fight and not care about anything or anyone. Jonas was good at that.

TWENTY-EIGHT

Tyler wished he knew where Ethan was. He was so cold and tired but refused to give up. He pushed aside branches and leaves. He knew the Miller was out there. He heard him run out of the mill when he escaped, and he was angry. Tyler still had his blood on his hands.

Tyler ran, pushing on through the burn in his legs. He needed to find Ethan and Kaitlyn. He knew he shouldn't, but he called out his lover's name. His voice was hoarse.

Tripping over a root, he crashed to the ground.

"Fuck," he groaned as he grabbed onto his aching knee.

Tyler sat up and leaned up against a tree. He wiped the sweat off his face and cleaned his glasses on his sweater. He grabbed onto the tree and pulled himself up. Now where was he supposed to go. He turned around.

Thud!

The sickle dug its blade deep into the tree. Tyler screamed as he came face-to-face with the Miller. His one good eye was filled with anger. He ripped the sickle out of the tree, and Tyler ran. The Miller chased after him, his eye focused on the young man.

"Help! Someone help!"

Tyler couldn't help but scream as he ran through the woods. He pushed aside more branches and dived beneath a large root that had come out from the ground, crawling beneath it like a small cave. He jumped back up and ran.

Rabbitface didn't give up. He was relentless as he chased after his intended victim. He swung his sickle tearing apart the branches. Tyler didn't dare to look back. The Miller's heavy boots stomped the dirt away. He growled running after Tyler. Like a rabies infected animal, he drooled from the mouth and charged for his prey. The Miller was hungry. His stomach growled, and his blood boiled. Tyler could sense the aggression. He had never seen so much in his life, even worse than his father's. From one nightmare, he escaped into another.

He could hear the Miller getting closer. Tyler came up to a fallen tree and he dived over it. He crushed himself next to the tree, letting his body sink into the mud. The Miller sniffed around, and Tyler covered his mouth with both hands. He closed his eyes tried to control his heavy breathes. Tyler wanted to pray but he couldn't remember any prayers. None except for one.

Now I lay me down to sleep,
I pray the lord my soul to keep.
If I should die before I wake,
I pray the lord my soul to take.

Silence. Tyler wanted to open his eyes, but he was afraid. What would he see when he did? Slowly he took his hands away from his quivering lips. Tears stained his cheeks. He opened his eyes saw nothing but the trees above. He raised his head over the fallen tree and screamed as the sickle crashed down centimeters from his face. He backed away, his hands sinking into the mud. The Miller pounced for him. Tyler screamed digging into the ground, wrapping his hand around the biggest rock he could find. With a throaty scream, he smashed the rock over the Miller's head.

Tyler got up and continued to run. If his father was here, he'd say to stop being a fag and to go back and fight. I can't do that! He pushed the voice out of his head and ran. He bolted through those thick woods. He sprinted until he came upon a clearing. He stopped dead in his tracks.

"No," he cried as he covered his mouth with both of his hands. He might have alerted the Miller where he was, but he couldn't care less.

On the ground was a body. A body wearing a plaid flannel shirt. A blue and black plaid flannel shirt. Tyler ran to the young man on the ground and fell to his knees. This couldn't be Ethan. Something had to be wrong.

Please let this be a nightmare, he silently prayed.

"Ethan," he cried. He ran his hand across the light stubble of his still beautiful face. Even covered in dirt and blood, he was perfect to Tyler. "Ethan, please. Wake up. You can't be dead."

Ethan's eyelids fluttered open, barely. Tyler smiled, pulling Ethan's head onto his lap. Ethan groaned in pain. Blood gored out of his open wound in his stomach.

"Tyler," he choked out. The one word sent him onto a coughing fit with blood spattering Tyler's face. Ethan tried to smile, but it turned into a wince, as pain shot through his entire body.

"Ethan, don't talk. I'm gonna get you help."

Tyler took off his sweater and applied it to Ethan's chest. He pushed down hard onto the wound and grabbed

Ethan's hands, placing them underneath his own. His blood turned the crimson sweater a dark shade of burgundy. The blood wouldn't end. Come on! Please, this cannot be happening. You cannot take him away from me.

Ethan grabbed onto Tyler's hand, clasping his fingers in his. He shook his head. Ethan knew there was no help for him. He was going to die, but he wanted...he needed Tyler to survive. Tyler was stronger than he'd ever give himself credit for, but Ethan always knew. Tyler was a survivor.

"Soon we will be out of these woods and we will be able to live our new life together. We will find the others. Kaitlyn, Billy, Jonas. They are still out there with the fucker who did this to you."

Ethan's eyes grew wide as he clawed at Tyler's arms. He coughed up blood.

"Ethan, please don't move. You're losing too much blood."

Ethan shook his head and convulsed in his lap. What was going on? Tyler didn't know what to do. Ethan squeezed Tyler's hand. Tyler kissed his forehead and cupped his face with his other hand.

"Ethan, please stop. It will be okay."

"Don't," he coughed, "Jonas." The words were light, barely audible.

"What about Jonas?"

Ethan held a fist up and opened up his fingers. Jonas's watch sat there in his palm. The same watch Jonas worshipped. Why did he have the man's watch?

"How?"

Why the Hell did he have Jonas's watch? Ethan didn't want to believe it. He refused to believe it. None of this made any sense to him.

"Jonas did this," Ethan whispered, his eyes growing

heavy. The pain seared his body like a fire. Keeping his eyes open was becoming a burden.

"No, Ethan, he couldn't." Could Jonas really have done this to his boyfriend? He was cruel, but he wasn't evil.

"Don't trust him," Ethan dictated. He pushed the watch into Tyler's hands. "Jonas." Ethan continued to cough, his eyes rolling back.

"Please, don't leave me," Tyler begged. He threw the watch to the ground and held Ethan's head with both hands.

Ethan's body convulsed.

Then he was still.

His head fell to the side and his dark eyes sat there wide and unblinking.

"Ethan?" Tyler whispered. He shook his body. "Ethan, wake up. Please wake up! I love you. Don't leave me. Ethan!" Tyler's sobs echoed through the woods. He no longer cared who heard him. This couldn't be the end. He had to wake up. But his eyes were open. He hugged Ethan's body close to his head and breathed in the scent of his hair.

He slammed his lips onto Ethan's and kissed him hard, but he was gone.

"Fuck," Tyler screamed, his voice echoing in the darkness.

Tyler clenched his fists and screamed, slamming his fists against his head. He pulled at his hair and screamed, his salty tears sliding into his mouth. He kept screaming and cursing until nothing came out of his opened mouth except for spit. He wished he was dead.

He looked down at Ethan's corpse and wanted the Miller to appear to end it all. He wanted to be with him. Together. Forever. Just like they promised.

This was his fault. If Tyler hadn't been involved with

Ethan. If he hadn't been found by his father in bed with him. If Ethan never knew him...none of this would have happened. Tyler might have well killed Ethan himself.

"I'm so sorry, Ethan. I'm so sorry," Tyler sobbed. He kissed his lips again and continued to apologize between kisses. He wanted Ethan to move. He wanted him to wake up. He wasn't dead. He wasn't dead. Tyler's sobs echoed in the night, and he knew the Miller would hear him soon. He looked down and closed Ethan's eyes.

"There you go, now you're asleep."

He wanted to die so badly. What did he have to live for? He had no home. No money. No family.

No Ethan.

He wished for death like he never had before. He brushed his fingers through dirty brown hair. No longer would he respond to Tyler's touch. Tyler didn't want to move. His mind said he had to, but his heavy heart weighed him down. A weight sat on his chest. It might as well be the Miller's sickle, which tore his love down.

The silver of the watch caught his eye and he picked it back up in his hand. He held it so tight, it marked his skin, leaving an outline of the watch on his palm. Who was the true villain here, Tyler wondered?

As he looked at the watch, his sadness gave way to a new feeling. A fury entered his body. A fury so strong it took over his mind and heart. All other thoughts left him and now he only wanted one thing. No, he didn't want to die. He thirsted for revenge.

He wanted to rip those assholes apart.

"It'll be okay, Ethan. We will be fine. I'm gonna get us out of here. We will be together forever just like we planned."

Tyler smiled. "Just sleep and I will be back, okay, my love?"

They were going to be together forever. Ethan promised him. Ethan never broke his promises.

He looked down at and kissed the bloody cold lips of his lover. Tyler pocketed the watch and wiped his tears away. He grabbed the necklace around his neck. The silver skeleton key Ethan gave him. The key that opened the door to their sanctuary. Tyler took off Ethan's silver ring and placed it on his left ring finger, like a husband saying I do on his wedding day. He kissed his lips and told him he loved him one last time before standing up.

No more tears came, but his breathing grew course and haggard. A flame had erupted in his heart, and there was no putting it out.

"Ethan, I won't let it end this way. I promise you, they won't get away with this."

On the ground he found the machete. Tyler lifted it in the air and turned around, taking one last look at the love of his life.

"I will be back for you. I promise."

Tyler turned around and walked away, no longer the same scared boy that had entered those woods only a few hours ago. In his place a feral beast was taking over, and it thirsted for blood. The sweet Tyler Wuerth was gone. He died along with Ethan in those woods. Jonas and that fucking monster were going pay. They were going to fucking pay. Tyler would make sure of that.

Tyler marched back towards the grist mill.

TWENTY-NINE

Kaitlyn felt as if she had been wondering the woods for hours. She didn't want to be alone anymore. She was never afraid of being alone. Even as a child, she loved being alone, but now the quiet had become something depraved, corrupting something she always found to be a pleasure.

Her walk was slow, barely a pace. She couldn't run anymore, but she couldn't let herself stop moving. In the distance she saw a light break through the trees. A smile came to her face. Was she saved? Oh God, please let this mean the nightmare is almost over. Kaitlyn jogged towards the light. It grew larger, more luminescent and as she came out of the woods, she found herself at a road. She saw a streetlight. She was joyous, nearly forgetting all that had taken place over the past couple hours. A road. She was out of the woods.

And she heard a car. Her nightmare was almost over. The headlights grew closer and Kaitlyn used her strength to run into the road. She waved her hands in the air. She screamed for help, thanking God for sending this for her.

She can get to the police and send help for the others. They would all be rescued, or at least what was left of them would be rescued.

The car swerved around her and kept going.

"No! Come back," she screamed. The smile fell, and she came down to her knees. "You asshole! Fuck you!"

A hand grabbed her shoulder and she screamed.

"It's me."

She turned around and found Tyler. She stood up and stared at the sight. Tyler's light blue button-up shirt and khakis were covered in blood. His blonde hair was dirty and stained red. He held a machete in his hand.

"Tyler, what happened? Are you okay?"

Kaitlyn looked and saw his eyes empty. The emotional boy she had met the other day wasn't standing before her. This was a shell. The soul had been torn out.

"Ethan..."

"Tyler, I'm so sorry." She knew what he was going to say. She didn't want him to finish.

"He's dead."

He was in shock. Tyler was looking at her, but he wasn't seeing her. He was looking past her. Kaitlyn hugged the boy. "Let's get out of here," she said.

"I'm going back to the grist mill."

"What? That's crazy. Tyler let's keep walking up the road. We can find help or a gas station."

He let go of her and shook his head.

"I can't. I'm going to kill him."

She couldn't believe her ears. Tyler was like a scared mouse and now he was a lion on the prowl. What he was saying was crazy. She couldn't let him go back to the grist mill. Not with all that had happened.

"I'm not letting you."

"Kaitlyn, you have to let me do this."

Kaitlyn heard the defiance in his voice. He wasn't going to budge. She took a deep breath and closed her eyes. Over such a short amount of time, she had grown to care for him so much, and she couldn't part with him like this. He was walking to his death.

"Fine, but I'm coming with you."

"No! I'm not going to let you die to. I already failed Ethan, and I won't fail you too."

Kaitlyn shook her head. "Oh Tyler, you didn't fail him. You didn't do anything wrong."

He ignored what she said. He didn't believe a word. If it wasn't for him, Ethan would be alive and that was a fact. He didn't want to be the cause of another death.

"Please go, Kaitlyn."

"No. I'm coming with you. I can be stubborn too."

Tyler nodded. There was no changing her mind. Together they walked back towards the grist mill. Tyler didn't know the way, but he felt he was going in the right direction. Something told him, he was meant to be back there, and eventually they found their way. Their walk was in silence, with Kaitlyn by his side the entire time.

"Are you sure?" Kaitlyn asked.

Tyler nodded, and the two entered the Cedar Creek Grist Mill once again. The bodies were already beginning to smell, and flies zipped around the hot room. They sat on the ground and rested. The fire was still going. Tyler sat beside it and felt his blood-caked flesh cooking. He held the machete in his lap and stared down at it. He ran his finger over the side, feeling the sharpness. The Miller definitely kept his tools sharp.

"There are more tools in the next room."

Kaitlyn nodded and walked through the door and found

the wall with them. She grabbed the pitchfork off the wall and sat beside the fire with Tyler. They sat in silence and waited. Retribution or death, neither knew. But they knew something was coming to an end soon.

The door burst open, and in came Jonas and Billy. Tyler stood up, leaving the machete on the ground.

"What are you doing here?" Tyler demanded.

"We ran in a giant fucking circle. Why the Hell are you?"

Tyler didn't answer. Kaitlyn stood up and felt the air grow tense. Tyler stared Jonas down, eyes locking on his. Billy didn't want to be anywhere near his father and walked towards Kaitlyn. Tyler walked towards Jonas.

"It's just us four," Jonas said.

"How do you know?" Tyler inquired. "What about Ethan?"

Kaitlyn and Billy stared at Tyler and Jonas. Their eyes were narrowed, almost ready to attack one another. Each man looking as wild as Rabbitface.

"Ethan? What about him?"

"I'm asking, how do you know it's only the four of us."

"Your friend didn't make it."

Tyler bit his lip and blinked back his tears. "You saw him die?"

Liar.

Jonas looked away as Billy wiped away his tears. Billy looked at the ground, unable to handle his father's lies. He looked over at the fire.

"Yes."

Liar.

"So, you watched him die. You were there as he died," Tyler pressured on.

Jonas gritted his teeth, "I said yes! Why the fuck are you interviewing me, kid?"

"Okay," Tyler answered. He knew the truth and it didn't matter what Jonas told him.

"What do we do now?" Billy asked.

Kaitlyn smiled down at the child. "I don't know. We wait?"

"Thank you."

Kaitlyn raised an eyebrow. "For what?"

"Not talking to me like a child and giving me an honest answer."

She hugged him close. "I'm scared," she admitted.

She leaned the pitchfork against the wall.

"Me too."

"That psychopath won't get you."

"Which one?" Billy quipped.

Kaitlyn was caught by surprise at his response. What did he mean by that?

"Hm?" The boy didn't reply. Outside, the Miller passed by the window looking in. All four in one place, waiting for him. He could hear his animalistic walk.

"Kaitlyn, get Billy out of here. There is a window upstairs. Go," Tyler ordered.

She nodded and grabbed the boy's hand, moving towards the next room.

"Where are you going with my child?"

"He's out there," Tyler whispered.

"Yeah, how do you know?" Jonas has had enough. He's been bossed around by two faggots tonight, and it was time for it to end. Jonas walked up to Tyler and poked him in the chest.

"I'm not afraid of you, kid."

"Well you should be."

In the doorway stood the Miller. Kaitlyn grabbed Billy's hand and the two ran into the next room and climbed the ladder. Kaitlyn tried not to gag at the sight of the corpses. She had to get Billy out of there. She kicked out the small square window, and helped Billy get down, before crawling out after. She fell to the ground. Billy helped her up and the two walked away from the mill.

Inside, Jonas and Tyler stared at the Miller. Tyler stared at the Miller's bloody mask. He could see his cold dark eye through the small hole. He was no monster. He was just a human being. He could die. Tyler smirked. He was going to kill him. Tyler grabbed the machete and held it up. Jonas eyed it. Where did he get that? But he didn't have much time to think as the Miller jumped for them. Tyler screamed and swung the machete. The Miller moved to the side and swung his sickle. Tyler ducked beneath it and as it came back around, he jumped back. The sickle missed his stomach, but grabbed at his shirt, ripped it. Tyler ran at the Miller, but he grabbed him by the throat and threw him across the room. Tyler hit the wall and slid to the ground. The machete was stuck in the floorboard, standing up like the sword in the stone.

He stepped up and gave the Miller a bloody smile.

"Is that the best you can do, you ugly fuck?"

Tyler raced for the machete and pulled it out, cracking the floorboard. He sliced the Miller's let. He ran past him and fell to his knees, sliding across the wooden floor as Rabbitface wielded his weapon and swiped. Tyler looked up as the sickle nearly grazed the tip of his nose, missing it only by a hair.

Jonas watched the fight between the two men. He had to get out of here. Fuck the kid! He had to run. Tyler stood up, but Jonas ran for the door, pushing the boy to the ground. Tyler eyed the cracked floorboard the machete created. Jonas's foot went right through and he screamed, unable to pull his foot out. He yanked at his leg, but it was stuck. Tyler stood up and the Miller watched the two men, eyeing who he should go after first.

"Help me," the older man screamed. Jonas didn't want to die. He couldn't die. His boy was still out there. Billy needed him.

Tyler watched as his dirty brown hair fell into his deer-like eyes. Sweat soaked his face. Tyler stood still as the Miller started to walk towards Jonas. Jonas shook his head.

"Boy, please help me!"

Tyler said nothing. He stood in place and tried not to smile as the Miller eyed the dirty asshole on the ground.

"Don't just stand there. Help me!"

Tyler lifted up the machete, and the Miller stopped and stared. His good eye looked confused as he looked on.

Tyler reached into his pocket and felt the cold metal of the expensive watch.

"What the fuck are you doing?"

Tyler didn't say anything. Tyler pulled the watch out and Jonas gasped.

"Listen to me, it was an accident. I couldn't do anything to help," he shouted, desperation in his voice. Jonas cried out as he continued to try and pry his foot out. Tyler swung the machete down. Jonas covered his face but was met by the sound of metal on wood. He moved his hands away and found the machete standing before him. The Miller stood behind Jonas, sickle in hand. Tyler said nothing. He threw the watch onto the ground, it landing right by Jonas. Tyler turned around and walked towards the door.

"You can't do this! I'm sorry!"

Tyler turned around and took one last look. "Save yourself."

Tyler exited the grist mill and slammed the door shut.

As screams filled the air, Tyler fell to his knees and cried. His sobs blended with the screams, creating a macabre symphony that only the Devil would enjoy.

His tears gave way to giggles. Crazy insane giggles. His laughter drowned out the screams, an insane screaming laughter. What did he just do? He just left that man for dead. But he deserved it. He killed Ethan, not Tyler.

Kaitlyn and Billy ran up to Tyler and they both stared at him. They were afraid of him. Kaitlyn hugged the child to her side as he cried.

"Where's Dad?"

Tyler stopped laughing and looked into the boy's big green eyes. He didn't know how to answer that. Inside the mill, Rabbitface has ripped the man apart, chopping him apart limb by limb. His body parts were strung around the room like Christmas decorations.

Kaitlyn helped Tyler up and hugged him. She brought Billy into the hug as well. It was time for them all to get out of here. With the boy in the middle, Tyler and Kaitlyn each held onto a hand and walked away from the mill. They didn't have time to waste.

The Miller stood by the fire and gazed at the pitchfork. He grabbed it in his hands and held it up.

Outside, the survivors walked back towards the woods, but before any of them could enter those woods, a scream broke their silent celebration of survival. Blood sprayed the ground as the body fell to the earth.

THIRTY

The Miller ran out of the doorway and threw the pitchfork. It torpedoed through the air and entered his victim's back. Blood splattered Tyler and Kaitlyn, as the young boy fell to the ground. The pitchfork sat in his back like a sword in a sheath.

Tyler screamed. He was only a child. He didn't deserve this fate. He was so innocent. So young. Kaitlyn turned around and stared at Rabbitface.

"Fuck you!"

She pulled the pitchfork out of the little boy's body and ran for the Miller. Tyler ran after her. She swung the pitchfork and stuck him in the leg. He yelped but grabbed Kaitlyn and threw her to the ground. He ripped the pitchfork out of his leg and held it up. He brought it down as Kaitlyn rolled away. Tyler helped her up, but the Miller impaled the farm tool deep into Kaitlyn's stomach. Tyler screamed.

"No!"

Blood poured out of her mouth.

"Run," she barked. She turned towards the Miller and smiled. She spit blood at him. "Burn in Hell, motherfucker."

The Miller pushed the pitchfork in deeper, the prongs ripping through the skin of her back. Kaitlyn felt only the burning pain as her body went limp on the pitchfork.

Tyler ran. He went for the woods and didn't turn around. As he raced through the woods, all he could think was that he was alone.

Alone.

The word repeated in his mind like a broken record. It was a blinking neon sign in his head. What would he do now? He had no one to help him. It was just him and the Miller now. Tyler ran until he hit the road. He stopped to look around, but not even the hint of a car was heard. He ran across the street and back into the woods. The Miller wasn't far behind. He was a wild bull running loose.

Tyler had to think. What should he do? What could he do? He had no time to stop and barely anytime to think. He could only focus on one thing: survival, so he kept on running. The Miller kept his focus on his prey. He ran with a limp, but his rage kept him going.

Tyler ran up to a large tree with a low hanging branch. He hid behind the tree and grabbed onto the branch, pulling it back. As the Miller passed the tree, Tyler let go and watched as the branch swung back into the Miller's face. Like a slingshot, it launched the Miller to the ground. Tyler looked at the predator and laughed.

"Fuck you!"

He ran away from the scene. He bought himself some time, it might only be a few seconds, but he mustn't waste it. He had to get help. He had to escape. This nightmare had to come to an end. He couldn't die in vain. He must live for Ethan.

After running for so long, Tyler eventually found his way out of the woods. He came upon a cornfield with a trail to the right. He looked back and didn't see Rabbitface. He limped down the trailer, passing a mailbox. The name was faded, but he could make it out—Hawkins.

"Miss Hawkins," he whispered to himself. "Miss Hawkins," he said again, this time screaming. Had salvation finally found him? The kind old lady lived on the edge of town, and he found her house. He didn't know how long he has been running, but it was no longer important. He was going to be safe soon.

The Miller darted out of the woods and with a scream, Tyler sprinted towards the house. He screamed for help and called the old woman's name. The Miller chased after him. Tyler ran up the stairs of her porch and threw himself at the door. He pounded his fists on the wooden door. He looked back and saw the Miller walking towards him. Tyler screamed so loud, his voice grew hoarse. It was nearly gone. He slammed his fists against the door. Miss Hawkins had to open up the door.

The door finally opened, and the elderly woman stared at him with giant eyes and a hand up to her mouth.

"What in the world? Tyler?"

"Help...me," he breathed.

Miss Hawkins nodded and helped him inside the house. She locked the door. The Miller stopped walking and stood outside, staring at the door. He paced back and forth and continued to watch the door. He left the front yard and circled the house.

Inside Miss Hawkins sat down beside Tyler on the sofa. She hugged him close. She didn't care that he stained her fluffy pink bathrobe. She had been asleep in bet when he came upon her home.

"What happened?" she asked.

Tyler cried. "Everyone is dead."

"Tyler," she spoke calmly, "who is dead?"

Tyler shook his head. He didn't want to go on. He wanted to sink into the sofa and sleep until the police got here. She needed to call them.

"The police, you need to call them," he begged. "Ethan, Kaitlyn...they're all dead. Oh God," he whimpered.

"Wait here, I'm going to call right now."

"Thank you, Miss Hawkins."

"Please, call me Vera."

Tyler nodded and leaned his head back onto the cushions. He closed his eyes and took in the comfort of the couch. He sunk into the soft material as he listened to his savior call the police on the phone.

It would all be over soon. The police would come and take him away to safety. Maybe they'd kill the asshole. As he thought about that, Tyler did have to ponder, where exactly was Rabbitface? At the grist mill, he had no trouble breaking down the door to get inside.

Tyler opened his eyes. Why didn't he break down the front door? Vera entered the room again, with a glass of water in her hand.

"I got you a drink. You must be thirsty."

"It's okay. Thank you."

She smiled and handed him the glass, forcing it into his hands. "Please take a sip. Your voice sounds horrible."

Tyler nodded and brought the glass to his lips. He tilted the glass back, but kept his lips closed. Something was telling him this wasn't right. Something was off. He set the glass down on the coffee table. Vera stared down at him, a smile on her face. The shadows of the room bathed her face, making her smile seem almost demonic. Behind the old woman, the Miller appeared in the dark.

Tyler screamed. Vera turned around and shrieked. Tyler stood up and grabbed her arm.

"We have to go!"

She looked at Tyler, and she wasn't screaming anymore. No, she was laughing. He knew it. He knew this wasn't right, and he had entered the trap like a fly stuck to a spider's web. She grabbed a small statue from the table and swung it across his temple. Before Tyler blacked out, he saw the Miller standing beside the old bitch watching him.

WHEN TYLER AWOKE, everything hurt. His body, his head, his heart. Everyone was dead, he knew. He was hoping to have woken up from a nightmare, but instead found himself back in Hell. He tried to move, but he couldn't budge. He opened his eyes, the bright lights burning his pupils. He was at a kitchen table with a plate set in front of him. His wrists were tied to the arm chair and his ankles were tied together. Blood dripped into his eyes, but all he could do was try and blink it away. One of his lenses was cracked. Miss Hawkins walked in and smiled at her guest.

"Oh, good you're awake," she spoke.

"What is going on?" Tyler asked. His voice was soft and confused.

"We are about to settle down for dinner. You're my guest. My son and I wanted to enjoy some company."

"Son?"

Vera smiled and looked over at Rabbitface. He wore a noose around his neck now, which she held onto, like a dog leash.

"Jack, he's a sweet boy. He's always been good to Mommy."

The Miller placed his head on her shoulder and she rubbed her hand through his dirty hair.

"Jack, go to your cage. This isn't a story for your ears." The crazy bitch smiled, showing off her yellow wretched teeth. She kissed his forehead and sent him off. She sat down at the table and looked up at Tyler.

Tyler watched as Jack entered a large animal cage in the corner of the room. He couldn't believe his eyes as the grown muscular man with the disgusting rabbit mask kneeled down in the cage and sat like a dog.

"You see, Jack wasn't always my boy."

"You kidnapped him?"

Vera laughed. "I didn't kidnap him. He was born to me!"

CHAPTER

THIRTY-ONE

T*wenty-Seven Years Ago*

VERA HAWKINS STRETCHED her limbs outside her small home. She was forty-four and beautiful. Her hair was dark and her eyes an emerald green that stood out from her pale white skin. She breathed in the hot Texas heat and wiped the sweat from her forehead. She stood by a clothesline and pulled folded clothes out of a basket and clipped them to the line. A soft wind blew the clothes in her direction. There was nothing lovelier than a warm summer breeze. She finished hanging her clothing and walked back into the small house. It was quiet as she sat on the couch. She organized the coffee table. Everything had to be perfect. What would happen if she had a guest over? She would never want anyone to think her to be a slob. That would be disastrous.

She sat down on the vintage love seat, but before she

could grab the book off the coffee table, the doorbell rang. The little jingle sounded throughout the house. Vera stood up and flattened her dress and walked to the front door. She slightly opened the door and looked through the crack and found a young pregnant woman in an ankle length floral dress. She held onto her stomach.

"I'm so sorry, ma'am. My car broke down outside your house. Could I use your phone?"

"Of course, come on in," Vera said, inviting the young woman in. She opened the door wider, and the twenty-something redhead entered the house. Her hair was a flaming red, dyed. Her dark roots were coming through. She waddled through the foyer, holding onto her large round belly. She looked as if she could pop any moment. The woman took in Vera's home, so immaculate.

"You have a lovely home."

"Thank you, Dear," Vera replied with a wide toothy smile.

"Ma'am?"

"Vera Hawkins. Please call me Vera."

"Okay, thank you so much, Vera. I'm Karen."

"It's lovely to meet you, Karen." Karen followed Vera into the living room as the two strangers sat down on opposite sides of the coffee table. An old rotary phone sat on the small table, next to Vera's book and a vase of freshly picked flowers. "Would you like a cup of tea?"

Karen smiled, thinking she had broken down outside the right house. She has had a long day already and a nice cup of tea seemed like the perfect medicine. She told her husband countless times her Oldsmobile could make the trip. He would tell her he'd buy her a new car and she constantly defended it, but now it seems her husband would have the last laugh.

"You can use the phone and I will go make us a nice spot of tea."

Vera walked down the hallway attached to the side of the living room and came into the kitchen. She lit a fire on the stove with a long match she kept by the side and placed a kettle over the flame. In the living room, Karen dialed zero and asked the operator to speak to a towing company. While Karen spoke on the phone, Vera set out two tea cups and saucers on the small round kitchen table. She listened as the young woman spoke on the phone. It has been so long since she has had company. She felt blessed.

The kettle whistled, and she called out for her new guest. Karen walked into the kitchen and sat at the table, as Vera poured the boiling hot water over the teabags.

"Thank you, Miss Hawkins."

"Please, call me Vera."

"Okay, I will. Your home is truly lovely. How long have you lived her?"

"Forty-four years. I was born in this house, as was my mother. I grew up in this house. I got married here and had my child here. This house has a lot of history for my family and I."

"That's amazing! I would love to start a life like that with my husband."

"I'm sure you will. Family is so important."

"Where are your husband and child now, if you don't mind me asking?" Karen asked as she brought the teacup to her lips. Vera's smile dropped, and Karen suddenly regretted her question.

"They both passed," Vera answered.

Karen gasped and covered her mouth. She couldn't imagine losing a child. Her baby wasn't born yet, and she already loved him so much.

"I am so sorry for your loss," Karen apologized.

"It's okay, Dear. Drink your tea. No one likes cold tea."

Karen finished off her tea and Vera poured her another cup. She rubbed her belly as she felt like someone was hitting her stomach with a hammer.

"He is a real kicker," Karen joked.

"That's the sigh of a healthy baby. You're having a boy?"

"Yes, I am. Joshua. Joshua Matthew Dunne."

"That's a lovely name, Karen. My son was named Jack."

"My father's name was Joshua. He passed when I was a little girl. I was about four or five when the Cancer got him."

Vera reached for her hand over the table and squeezed it. "I am sorry to hear that. I feel as if God brought us together today."

Karen smiled, liking the idea.

"Where were you heading?" Vera inquired.

"I have family in Colorado."

"And your husband? Where is he?"

Karen finished off another cup of the tea tied her hair back in a ponytail. It was a hot summer day and as nice as the woman's home was, there didn't seem to be air conditioning. It felt hotter than a stove in here.

"Tony, that's my husband, is in the army. He is stationed in Australia right now as we speak." She grimaced as her future son kicked up another storm at her insides.

"You are so lucky to have God bless you with the gift of motherhood. You are holding the miracle of life within you."

Karen never believed in God as a teenager, but now that she was twenty-nine years old, she believed in a greater being. Something out there had to have helped her get at this point in her life. Five years ago, she was estranged from her family, homeless, and addicted to heroin. But then something brought Tony into her life. He helped her get clean and over the next five years they fell in love, married, and now they were expecting their first child.

"Do you want to feel, Vera?"

"Really?" The older woman's face beamed up, like a child's face on their birthday.

Karen nodded. Vera stood up and bent down beside Karen. She bit her bottom lip as she placed her hands on Karen's stomach. Vera's heart raced as she waited. Nothing was happening. As she was about to give up, she felt the kick.

"I felt him! I felt little Jack," Vera exclaimed.

"Joshua."

"What was that?" Vera looked up at Karen with her big green eyes.

"The baby's name is Joshua. You called him Jack."

"I am so sorry. I was thinking of my...never mind."

Karen felt bad for her. She seemed like a lonely woman who needed a friend. She was like that once too.

Vera placed an ear against Karen's belly and gripped tighter onto her stomach. She listened to the kicking and smiled.

"Miss Hawkins?"

Vera grabbed onto the skin, her nails digging in.

"Vera, stop! You're hurting me!"

Karen stood up, pushing Vera away. Vera sat on her butt sprawled out on the linoleum floor of the kitchen.

"Um, where is the restroom?"

"Next room, door to the left."

Karen walked out of the kitchen and down the hall into the bathroom. She locked herself in the restroom. A cold chill ran up her spine. She no longer felt warm. A different kind of sweat slipped down her face. It no longer felt right to be there. She prayed the tow truck would get there soon. She flushed the toilet and washed her hands, splashing cold water onto her face. Once she left, she never had to turn back again. She would be in Colorado with her family in no time. She was planning to stay there until the baby came. Joshua was due to enter the world in the next few weeks.

As she left the bathroom, a smell caught her nose. She contorted her face and groaned. It smelled like a rotting animal in the hallway. She followed the pungent smell and found herself outside of a slightly opened door. She pushed it open and found Vera's bedroom. A lump was asleep beneath the blanket.

Vera said her husband died, if that is true, then who is this? Karen slowly walked up to the bed and shook the hard lump.

"Excuse me, are you okay?"

She pulled the blanket back and screamed. In the bed was the rotting corpse of a once-young man. A cockroach crawled out of his mouth and into the empty eye socket, where his left eye once stood. She backed away and felt a crib against her back. She slowly turned around and inside the crib was a dead infant. She covered her mouth and gasped. She backed away and felt along the walls. Her legs felt weak and she throat tasted of acid. She vomited onto the floor.

"I see you met my husband and son."

Karen turned around and wiped her mouth. Her lips shook and her breathing grew heavy.

"Vera, I think I will wait in my car." She pushed past the woman and walked back towards the foyer. "Thank you so much for your hospitality, but I have to go."

Vera narrowed her eyes. "Wait! Don't go! I need my

baby! I need Jack," she shrieked. The woman grew old in that instant as Karen noticed every wrinkle in her face. Vera grabbed onto Karen's thin bony arms and spun her around. "Don't you dare take my son away from me!"

"Karen pushed Vera to the ground. "Get the fuck away from me!" Karen hobbled towards the front door. She grabbed the knob, but before she could even turn it, Vera was racing at her with a hammer lifted high into the air. She brought the weapon down. Karen fell to the floor. The room seemed to spin, and her vision blurred. Her face grew wet with blood.

She groaned in pain. Her thighs were wet. This couldn't be happening to her.

"Oh God, no!" Not now! The baby could not come now. "Damn," she screamed. The baby was coming, and her water broke. Vera threw the hammer to the ground and bent down. She spread open Karen's legs and ripped off her underwear.

"Jack is coming. My boy is returning to me." Vera smiled as she stared at Karen's vagina.

"He is not Jack. Please don't hurt my baby," Karen begged. Tears ran down her face as she screamed in agony. For an hour, Karen prayed for God to save her and her son, and for an hour her prayers went unanswered.

"Something is wrong," Karen cried. She had to get out of there. She had to find a hospital. Something was wrong. Something wasn't right with the baby, but she couldn't move.

"It will be okay, Jack," Vera whispered to the belly. Vera stood up and walked towards the kitchen. Karen grabbed onto the doorknob and tried to stand up. Her legs shook and blood dripped down her inner legs. This couldn't be real. She had to be having a nightmare.

She fell to the ground and cried out in pain. Her eyes grew wide as Vera entered the foyer with a knife in hand. Karen backed away, using her elbows for strength.

"Don't worry, I just cleaned it. Jack won't be dirty."

"Please, don't. You don't have to do this," Karen cried. The pain grew unbearable. She screamed as her son tried to squeeze himself out of her vagina. Vera got onto the floor and spread open Karen's long legs.

"The umbilical cord I think is wrapped around his neck, Dear. I can fix this." Vera lifted up the knife. Karen shook her head and felt in that moment, God didn't give a damn about her. Vera brought the knife down into Karen's stomach. Karen screamed as a fire-like pain shot through her body.

"Don't," Karen weakly begged. She knew she was going to die, but she just wanted her son to be okay. Vera ignored her cries and sliced open her stomach, as if she was cutting a steak. She reached both hands in and dug deep inside her stomach and pulled the pregnant woman's organs out. Karen continued to scream, feeling Vera's bony fingers inside her stomach. Karen was praying again, but this time she was praying for death as she watched her murderer ripped out her insides.

Vera found the baby and pulled him out. Before Karen died, her intestines making a long trail down the hallway, she watched as Vera pulled the placenta off the baby and cut off his umbilical cord with the knife. *I love you*, Karen thought before giving into death.

Vera cradled the baby close to her breast and prayed for him to open his eyes.

"Please Jack, come back to me." She cradled the baby and hummed a tune her mother used to sing to her as a little girl. The baby opened his eyes and cried. Vera smiled. She was a mother again.

Vera held the baby close to her chest and wrapped him in a blanket. She would be a good mother to Jack. That is what she told herself. Sometimes children misbehaved, but not her son. He would be her good little boy. When he acted out, she would correct it. She would make sure he loved his mommy very much.

THIRTY-TWO

Vera finished her story and took a sip of water as she watched her guest. Tyler stared at her in disbelief. She licked her dirty rotten yellow teeth, or at least the ones that were left. Her stringy gray hair curled around her face like branches on a tree. As the fire roared behind her in the fireplace, she looked like a witch.

The Miller sat in his cramped cage and stared at Tyler. Tyler felt bad for the sick bastard.

"You look like him. I think that is why Jack has taken a liking to you?" Her gaze seemed far off. She was no longer in the kitchen sitting at the table.

"Who?" Tyler asked.

"He was a boy; Cody I believe his name was. Maybe Cory? The name doesn't matter, but he was an attractive young thing, like you. A faggot too. He had blonde hair and blue eyes as well. You really do look like him. Jack liked him. He liked him a lot. My son wasn't quite who he was now. He was sixteen, you know. Still a child with so much to learn. He's always been partial to pretty boys, like you."

"Jack was an awkward child. He was his mama's boy.

But that boy, Cody, nearly took him away from me. I even caught them kissing in the boy's car. They had been having an affair behind my back. Jack would walk into town and see that boy, and together they would spend time and do all kinds of things. I'm his mother. I know what is best for him."

"When I heard them speaking of being together. I thought Jack was going to leave me. I was devastated. I want you to know, I don't care if my son is a faggot, but no one takes my boy away from me, man or woman, so I killed that boy. I made Jack watch. I put him in this very cage and made him think about what he had done to his poor old mommy. And not only did I kill the boy, but I killed the entire family. The parents, I did, but the girl, I forced the knife into Jack's hand and pushed him into killing the girl. She was a pretty girl, with a pretty name. Ione, it was. I believe she was the boy's twin."

Tyler sat there and listened to the heinous tale she spun. He felt guilt for the man he called a monster. Taken from his mother and punished all his life, until he was this thing. What did she do to him to turn him into such an animal? He was barely a human anymore.

"Crazy bitch," he muttered.

Vera snapped out of her fantasy and glared at the young man.

"What did you say?"

"I said you're a crazy bitch."

Vera stood up and slapped him across the face so hard, he felt like his head was going to do a complete spin. He looked up at her and smiled. He tasted blood on his lip, and he spit it right into her face.

"Don't spread your disease!" She quickly grabbed a napkin and washed the spots of blood from her face. She grabbed a knife and held it to his throat. He was tied to the chair, but he didn't care. No way in Hell would he give into her.

She looked down at his body and smiled. She ripped open his shirt, the buttons falling to the ground. She ran her long bony fingers down his slim body, feeling the toned muscles in his body. Tyler bit his lip and closed his eyes. He tried to think of a happy place, but his only happy place was taken away from him and it was this bitch's fault!

"As I said, my special boy always liked the pretty boys like you."

She walked over to the cage and opened the door. She grabbed onto the rope around his neck and dragged the Miller across the room. The masked man squealed in pain as his mother threw him to the ground. Vera untied Tyler and cut the rope around his ankles.

Tyler pushed her away, but before he could even take a step, the Miller was on top of him. Together, mother and son dragged him back to the kitchen table and they tied his ankles to the back legs of the table and used rope to connect each wrist to the other two legs. His face was against the dirty table and his ass arched in the air.

Spread eagle, he was bent over the table, the wood digging into his bare stomach. Vera came up from behind him and grabbed his crotch and smiled. She turned to her son. "We've got a big boy over here!"

Tyler bit his lip and tried to fight back the tears. This couldn't be happening right now. Why wouldn't this nightmare just end for him? The depraved woman unbuckled his belt and whipped it out, throwing it to the ground. She pulled down his skintight khakis and let them hang around his ankles. He shivered as a chill blew through the opened window.

"Have fun with him, Jackie Boy." She turned towards Tyler. A kettle whistled in the kitchen. "I will be right back."

She disappeared into the next room. Tyler tried to move, but the knots were so tight he couldn't budge. The Miller came up from behind him and grabbed his neck. He licked Tyler's cheek. Tyler shuddered. His throat burned with the taste of bile. The Miller stuck a dirty hand into Tyler's briefs and grabbed his penis.

"Get the fuck away from me," he screamed.

The Miller slammed his head against the table and pulled down Tyler's briefs. His legs were spread so far apart.

"Please," Tyler begged.

The Miller looked down at his new play toy and tilted his head, like the wild dog he was forced to become. Tyler turned his head as much as he could and in the one eye, he saw confusion. It was fleeting, but Tyler felt a connection with him.

The Miller broke contact and the connection was gone. Tyler cried out as he felt The Miller enter him.

"Please stop," the boy cried.

The Miller groaned and growled like a wild animal. Tyler screamed as the Miller ripped into him. He couldn't stop his tears, as his rapist thrusted into him. Tyler grabbed onto his ropes and held onto them hard, trying to ignore the pain. He tried to fight back, but all he could do was close his eyes. He pictured Ethan's face. His beautiful face as he kissed him. He pictured Ethan making love to him. Not fucking him like this vicious animal, but really caring for his body.

Vera came back in with a cup of tea and watched the sight with a smile on her thin chapped lips. The Miller yelped and as he fucked his toy. Tyler was spent, losing the will to live. He cried for Ethan. He wanted to be with Ethan again.

When he finished, he Miller ran to his mother and hugged her. She kissed his head.

"You did good, boy." She looked over at Tyler. "You are a disgusting slut."

Tyler wished for death. Anything would be better than this. Spread over the table, pants on the ground. He had given himself to Ethan, and this savage animal took what was special away from him.

As the wrinkled beady-eyed woman smiled her cracked yellow teeth, Tyler felt the blood and cum dry on his legs. He no longer cared. It was hopeless. There was no way he could ever escape this situation. He was trapped in this god forsaken house with the fucked-up woman and son.

How could he escape? He was tied down to the table with his pants around his ankles. No matter how hard he fought, he would still be stuck there.

"Don't give up."

Tyler looked up. Who said that? Right next to him stood Ethan. Not the corpse but the Ethan he knew before this tragedy.

"You're dead. This isn't real."

"I'm real to you. I'm telling you not to give up. Keep fighting."

"I can't."

"Yes, you can! You need to keep fighting for me."

"Ethan, this is hopeless. I'm going to die."

"So then go out fighting."

Vera looked over, shrugging her shoulders.

"Who in Hell's name are you talking to?"

Tyler looked up at her and smiled. He felt a giggle bubbling up inside him. It escaped as Vera watched.

"The boy has lost it," she stated to her son. "Take him to the basement, Jack."

The Miller walked up to Tyler and undid the ropes. He grabbed onto the table as the Miller tried to lift him in the air. The boy screamed and cried. He lost grip on to the edge of the table, but he grabbed a kitchen knife.

He threw Tyler over his shoulder and walked towards the basement door. Tyler lifted up the knife and screamed as he brought the blade down into his back. The Miller let out an animal-like shrill. Tyler fell onto the ground. He looked up to see the fucker spinning in circles trying to reach for the knife. Tyler nearly laughed at the sight.

"Jack!" the crazy old bitch screamed as she ran towards her son. Tyler lifted up his underwear and pants. He charged for the front door as Vera pulled the knife out of her poor son's back. "How dare you!" Her voice sounded like the screeching of a kettle.

She ran at Tyler, knife in midair. He screamed as she impaled the weapon into his back shoulder. He spun around and struck the older woman. He struck her so hard across the face, she fell to the ground. She held onto her cheek, feeling the burn of the faggot's hand on her skin. How dare he touch her like that.

"Jack, get the pervert!"

Vera's son always did as he his mother asked. He walked up to Tyler and grabbed him by the hair and slammed his face against the wall. Tyler screamed as pain shot through his head. He grabbed Jack's arm and bit down, tasting the metallic blood from beneath his dirty flesh. The Miller cried out grabbing his arm. Blood dripped to the floor creating a crimson puddle.

"I'm going to kill you," Vera screamed as she jumped onto Tyler's back. She grabbed the handle of the knife, still resting in his back, and she twisted the blade. Tears came to his eyes as the pain became fire.

"Get off me, you old hag!"

Tyler backed into the wall and crushed Vera. She grabbed his neck, choking him. Instead of breathing, all he could do was cough. She held onto his neck with a grip so tight, his lungs burned, begging for air. He raced backwards to the wall, and Vera's arms loosed around his neck. She fell off his back and Tyler spun around.

Vera looked into his eyes, and something scared her as she stared right into his big blue eyes. The eyes that were once hopeless, were filled with rage. He reached over his shoulder and ripped the knife out of his shoulder, blood spilling down his back. He stared at Vera with a snake-like glare and he let out a primal scream as he swung the knife.

The Miller cried out for his mother as the knife entered her neck. A gasp escaped her lips. Tyler smiled as he ripped the knife out, tearing the skin. Blood spattered out from the vein he hit. The blood sprayed his face and bare torso.

"Jack," she gagged, her blood choking her.

Tyler swung the knife again. He screamed each time he swung the knife into her neck. Repeatedly he stabbed her, more and more blood spilling onto his hands. She fell to the ground, grabbing onto her neck, but Tyler wasn't done yet. He straddled her body and continued to stab the fucking bitch in the face.

She was dead, but Tyler couldn't stop himself. Something had taken him over. He was possessed and now he didn't know how to stop himself. He wasn't the same boy who ran away the night before. In his place was someone dark, someone crazed with want of revenge.

A muscular hand grabbed him by his neck and threw him across the room. Tyler's back landed on the stairs. His body throbbed as he tried to stand up. The Miller held onto his mother and cried loud sobs over her bloody corpse. Tyler bit his lip. *What did I just do?*

The Miller turned around, his eyes blacker than ever, and he charged like a wild bull. Tyler ran up the stairs. His abuser ran after him, screeching like a wild boar. He was hungry and Tyler wasn't prepared to be his meal. There was nowhere to run but he eyed the window. He had no time to think. Tyler dived through the window and flew through the air in a rain of glass. He plummeted through the branches of a nearby tree and fell to the ground, hard. He groaned as he tried to stand up. His arm pulsated in agony, while his ankle suffered from the fall. He looked over at his bicep and found a large shard of glass impaled into his skin. He closed his eyes and took a deep breathe. He grabbed onto the glass and slowly pulled it out, feeling his flesh open up.

"Fuck," he whimpered. His breathing grew hard, and all he could do was focus on that. The shard never seemed to end, and when it finally came out, he threw it to the ground. He looked up at the window and the Miller's revolting Rabbit face stared down at him. He turned around and disappeared from the window.

Tyler cursed the Hawkins family and he ran towards the cornfield with a limp in his run. Mostly shirtless and cold, Tyler only wanted to escape. He pushed aside the giant stalks of corn. He knew the Miller wouldn't be far behind, but where the Hell was he? Tyler had been concentrated on running, that he had no clue which direction the road was.

"Fuck."

Tyler stopped running to get his surroundings, but each direction was just more cornfield. Not even a damn trail. He held onto his arm and winced. The wound was bleeding profusely. He took off what was left of his shirt and tied it around his bicep. He groaned as he tightened his tourniquet. Blood instantly soaked through the shirt.

He started to walk. He no longer felt the burn in his lungs. He had been running for so long, he had become immune to the pain in his lungs. Pushing aside the cornstalks, he moved through the field. He had no idea where he was going, but as long as he got farther from the farmhouse, he was okay.

The Miller ran into the cornfield. He ran with a limp, but nothing would stop him now. Mommy was dead, and the boy took her away from him. Swinging his sickle, he tore through the large stalks.

Tyler limped through the thick field. His ankle burst with pain as he quickened his pace. He stopped and touched his ankle over his boot. Pain shot through his body. Damn it. I can't think about this now. I have to keep going. But where do I go?

Tyler quickened his paced and did his best to run. He looked back and ran right into a body. He fell onto the ground and cried out, waiting for the sickle to crash down into his body. He looked up and chuckled. It was a fucking scarecrow. Tyler stood up and touched the stomach, fearing it might come to life. Anything was possible for him now.

The Miller heard the rustle of the cornstalks and a scream. He lifted up his sickle and ran towards his target. He saw the body on the ground and he brought his sickle down, impaling it into the soft flesh of his victim. The Miller licked his lips, but as he brought out the sickle, there was no blood. It was the scarecrow. What had happened? His mind was a chaotic jumble of nothing. His brain was like a heavy fog. Rabbitface looked around, and Tyler came out of hiding and grabbed the noose and pulled. The

Miller's sickle fell to the ground. Tyler reached for the sickle and stabbed him in the chest. The Miller fell to the ground. Tyler nudged him with his foot, but he didn't move. Tyler sighed and turned around. He limped through the cornfield, but behind him, the Miller sat up and turned his head to look at Tyler. He pulled the sickle out of his own chest.

Tyler escaped the cornfield and entered back into the woods. He didn't run, no longer able to ignore the pain that rushed through his body. He shivered in the night, wishing Ethan was there to warm him up. But that will never happen again. Slowly, the Miller followed the boy.

Tyler came upon the road. Again, not a car in sight, so he went back into the woods on the other side. As he walked through the woods, Tyler felt the emotion well up inside. Every intense feeling grew so strong, he couldn't hold it back anymore. Tears fell down his face, while a sense of peace overtook him, but he had no idea, it would end soon, as the Miller was still alive and was following him.

He needed to sleep. Where was he to go after this? He had no home. No family. He leaned up against a tree and yawned. The crunch of a twig caught his attention. His eyes snapped back open and he looked around. No one was there. No other noise, but he ran. Through the woods, he ran, until he came out of them on the other side. He was back at the river and looked up at the building before him.

He was back at the grist mill, where the whole nightmare began. On the ground were Kaitlyn and Billy, and Tyler's heart sunk for them. They didn't deserve this. None of them did.

He didn't hear any other noises. Maybe he never heard anything at all? He entered the grist mill and shut the door. Jonas's body parts decorated the room like grisly Christmas decorations. He sat down by the fire, which was slowly dying. He let the hear warm his skin as he lied down on the floor and closed his eyes. Sleep. His eyes felt so heavy. He could sense the world of dreams coming upon him soon.

The door blew open and Tyler sat up. The wind howled, and no one stood there. Tyler eyed the machete still in the ground and he looked up at the doorway. Jonas's leg was still in the crevice of the floor. Tyler crawled towards the machete, keeping his eyes on the door. Slowly he made his way for the machete. He pulled it out and steadily stood up. He held the weapon up like a baseball bat and watched the doorway and waited. As he watched the entrance, the Miller limped out of the other room and watched the back of Tyler. Like a mouse, the Miller limped towards the boy.

Tyler breathed deeply and gripped the handle of the machete tightly. With a warrior cry, he spun around and swung the machete. Metal hit metal and the sickle fell to the ground.

One of them was going to die, and Tyler was prepared to fight. He swung the machete again. He was not leaving until one of them was dead. The third time, the machete contacted the Miller's chest, just slicing the surface as he moved back a second too late. The Miller shrieked. He was barely human and hardly an animal but stuck somewhere in between. One of his rabbit ears flopped down, while the other stood up. He looked at Tyler, while Tyler prepared to hit him again with his weapon. Both shirtless and covered in blood and dirt, neither man looked human anymore. They were feral creatures waiting to attack.

The Miller dived for his sickle, and Tyler ran into the next room of the grist mill. Rabbitface followed after and ran at Tyler and the boy charged right back towards him. He swung his machete, and the Miller sliced his sickle through the air. Tyler screamed as the sickle sliced him across the chest. His machete fell out of his hand and hit the wooden floor, the blade lodging itself deep into the ground, right by Jonas's head.

Blood dripped down his body. He rushed towards Rabbitface, his shoulder colliding with his stomach, and plowed him down to the ground. They both fell. The sickle slid across the wooden floor. The Miller grabbed Tyler's head and slammed it against the ground. The boy screamed as pain shot through his head. With each slam of his head, it felt like a jackhammer was working on his brain. Tyler kicked the fucker in the groin and the Miller growled grabbing his crotch. Tyler crawled away and kicked his attacker in the head. The Miller rolled onto his back and whimpered.

Tyler grabbed onto the machete, but it was stuck. Fuck! He needed something. Anything. He grabbed a large rock and lifted it over his head, but Rabbitface grabbed onto Tyler's leg and bit down. The rock fell from his hands as Tyler screamed. The Miller's teeth broke through his skin, all the way down to his bone. He kicked the Miller's head off of his leg and stepped back as The Miller grabbed his sickle and stood up. He was hunched over like a cat on the prowl.

Rabbitface grabbed his sickled ran for the boy, using his head against Tyler's stomach, taking all the wind out of him. They fell back to the ground. The Miller lifted up his sickle and swung it down. Tyler grabbed his wrist as the blade stood barely an inch above his eye. Shit, Tyler thought. His heart pounded faster in his chest as he held onto that wrist with all of his strength. He couldn't let the monster kill him.

He pushed his arm aside and bit into his wrist. The Miller snarled, and Tyler kicked him in the stomach. He flew back hitting the ground. The Miller stood up and ran at him with the sickle again. Tyler grabbed a large wooden beam and smacked it across the killer's face. He went down to the ground and the sickle flew across the room. The Miller crawled on top of Tyler and ripped the weapon out of his hand. He grabbed onto Tyler's wrists and held them over his head. He licked his lips. He sniffed Tyler's neck and licked it. Tyler wasn't sure if he was going to kill him or fuck him again.

Tyler smiled. "Come on, you ugly rabbit-faced mother fucker!"

The Miller lost his smile and wrapped his strong muscular hands around the boy's skinny throat. Rabbitface stood up and lifted his victim into the air by the neck. Tyler couldn't breathe. His lungs burned as if they were set on fire. The Miller's grasp was so strong, Tyler felt his neck was threatening to break any second. Tyler scratched and clawed at his predator's hands, but they became stronger the more he fought back. Rage filled the dark eye behind the mask. Black spots appeared before Tyler's eyes. The Miller was Mount Vesuvius and Tyler was Pompeii. With all his strength he picked up his hands and pushed his thumb into the Miller's bloody eye socket. He used as much pressure as he could. The Miller threw him down, with a painful yelp. Tyler coughed for air, trying to catch his breathe. The Miller grabbed him by the hair and dragged him across the floor towards an apple press. What was he about to do? Tyler fought against his hold, but the killer would not let go. The Miller shoved his head into the machine. Tyler felt the metal on top of his head. The Miller head him down with his foot and turned the wheel to push down what looked like a metal lid attached to a giant screw. Tyler screamed as the metal came closer and closer. He eyed the sickle on the ground and reached for it. The press was now tight on his head. Tyler felt like his head could explode like a grape. He reached for the sickle, but it was too far away. Come on, Tyler begged. It was only an inch out of his reach. He reached for the Miller's leg and tore at the wound in his leg. The Miller fell to the ground, screaming. Tyler pulled his head out and rubbed his temples.

The sickle sat in the middle of the floor and Tyler crawled for it. Jack grabbed his leg and pulled him back towards him. Tyler screamed, clawing at the floor, his index finger's nail being torn off. He cried out but could not focus on the pain in that moment. He kicked out, getting the fucker's hand off of his ankle. Both men sat up on all fours and stared directly at one another. The sickle sat between them as each grabbed the handle. The Miller barked in his face, and Tyler let out an angry scream into his, before punching him in the face. The Miller fell back, and Tyler held onto the sickle. Tyler backed away and watched the Miller sit up.

Enough was enough. With one last cry, Tyler ran at Jack Hawkins and brought the sickle down into his chest. He ripped it out and brought it down again.

Rabbitface looked up at Tyler and for a moment all he saw was fear. His good eye was big and round like a child's eye.

"Mommy," the Miller whimpered.

Jack Hawkins's voice cracked as he called out for the only woman to show him any love, or what he thought was love, but she was gone and now he was confused and alone.

For a moment, Tyler felt he couldn't kill Jack, but then an image of Ethan's corpse flashed before his eyes and with a guttural scream, he brought the sickle down into the Miller's chest. Tyler fell onto the ground, straddling the Miller, and brought the round blade again into the fucker's chest. Repeatedly he stabbed him. Blood splattered Tyler's crimson-stained face. He screamed each time he swung the weapon down.

Again.

Again.

Again.

His screams became fits of laughter. Once the Miller stopped moving, Tyler threw the sickle to the ground. His laughter died, and he stared down at the Miller's still body. Tyler stood up.

"Burn in Hell."

Tyler limped away from the body and exited the grist mill. He walked away and silently cried. The tears melted away the blood as his nightmare had finally come to an end.

Tyler limped through the woods. Alone, cold, bloody. Everything hurt. His muscles ached, and his heart felt numb. Everyone was dead. All those good people. And Ethan. Ethan had been taken away from him. He was dead. How could four little letters hold such power? D-E-A-D.

He came to a stop and began to cry. He couldn't stop himself. Everything was finally coming to him. They were all dead. He was alive. Dead. Alive. Dead. Dead. Dead.

But he was alive.

Ethan.

The love of his life was stolen from him and he was alone. Where did he go from here? He desperately wanted Ethan to be alive. He always knew what to do. But Tyler was here. Alone, but alive. He defeated the monster.

He fell to his knees. Tyler looked up at the moon that shined through the canopy of trees and let out a scream. He screamed until his throat hurt. His screaming gave way into heavy sobs. All emotion waterfalled out of his body.

Beneath the dark sky, one would never know Tyler had escaped Hell.

Tyler stood up and continued his trek. The branches no longer bit at him, but instead seemed to embrace him. You're alive, they said. Tyler pushed his cracked glasses up his nose and made out a small light in the distance

What is that? Is that a house? A car? I don't even know anymore. I feel as if I'm losing my mind.

The light grew larger and Tyler quicker his pace. What was that? He limped and limped, ignoring the burn in his body. He came out of the woods onto an empty road. The light was a streetlamp. He was still alone, but he was no longer lost.

He began to walk down the lonely stretch of road. He looked down the road and it seemed to disappear into the distance. He was walking deeper into the abyss. He has escaped Hell, but now he was entering the unknown. The only sounds he heard over the light pattering of his boots, was that of the wind that nestled his body.

He wouldn't give up. He was no longer a victim.

He was a survivor.

THE END

Acknowledgments

There are so many people I want to thank. I need to thank the rest of my family, my father Bill, my other brother Keith, and my sister Marlena. They are a great support system and have always been there to help me achieve my dreams. Thank you for having confidence in me.

Thank you to Kristine Henderson, who lets me use her tea shop, Infuse Tea Bar as a second home. I practically wrote this entire novel in her shop. Thank you to Richard Reyes (Instagram: alleged_art) for creating this amazing cover art. Thank you to Samantha for taking my headshots and being a great friend.

Thank you to Encompass Ink for believing in my work, and helping me get my book out into the world. It's been a dream working with you.

ABOUT THE AUTHOR

Bryan Michael Ellis was born on June 9, 1990, and grew up on Long Island, New York. He lived his entire life there except for his four years at SUNY New Paltz, where he graduated with a bachelor's degree in English. From an early age, Bryan had an overactive imagination and would use writing as an outlet for his ideas. He always knew he wanted to be a writer and is now fulfilling his dream. He is an avid tea drinker and animal lover, living with his rescue cat, Callie, who is the perfect writing partner. Growing up he had a big love of the horror genre. Horror movies, books, etc...he couldn't get enough of the genre, but he always felt one thing was lacking and that was representation of LGBT+ people. He never saw himself in any of the horror films or books he read and loved. Now Bryan spends his time writing (mostly) Horror novels with LGBT+ characters, hoping his readers feel included, and frightened.